Quicksilver

RICHARD L. GRAVES

Quicksilver

STEIN AND DAY/*Publishers*/New York

First published in 1976
Copyright © 1976 by Richard L. Graves
All rights reserved
Designed by David Miller
Printed in the United States of America
Stein and Day/*Publishers*/Scarborough House,
Briarcliff Manor, N.Y. 10510

Library of Congress Cataloging in Publication Data

Graves, Richard L
Quicksliver.

I. Title.

PZ4.G77557Qi   [PS3557.R289] 813'.5'4   75-35864
    ISBN 0-8128-1913-6

For Sally and Rick

The physicists have known sin;

and this is a knowledge which they cannot use.

—J. Robert Oppenheimer,
November 25, 1947

Contents

Quicksilver

Prologue

I

The *chola* bird whistled three times. In the canopy of rain forest sixty feet above, a band of red howler monkeys mocked the signal.

The headman wondered whether the foreign *ladinos* would notice the anomaly. The *chola* whistles only once, and then only after it has made its kill.

He scrutinized the leathery foliage on the other side of the trail and tightened his grip on the bone handle of his heavy machete. Nothing out of the ordinary. Good. When he moved, his companions would move, quickly.

For two days now, he and his band of six Quiché guerrillas had followed the five *ladinos* and their three heavily laden mules, pacing the little caravan on its route from the coastal plain into the highlands and, now, once again, down into the rain forest of the valley. The ground trembled faintly, and the headman shifted position. The gods are everywhere, he thought. He hoped they were smiling on this venture. His mind turned to the *ladinos*. They were foreigners, to be sure, probably enemy guerrillas supplied by the Cubans from over the sea. If that were the case, they would be carrying supplies and weapons, perhaps gold, on their mules.

In any event, they were climbing into the Quiché hills without having made arrangements beforehand. That made them enemies.

The headman glanced down at his automatic rifle,

supplied by the friendly round-eyed foreigner with hair the color of the howler monkeys. Perhaps the treasure of the mules would interest him.

The acrid smell of cigarette smoke reached the headman's nostrils. It was a good sign; the *ladinos* were approaching at their ease, unsuspecting. He squatted on his heels, immobile, coiled, his ears registering all the sounds of the rain forest.

The cigarette smell was close now.

A moment later he heard the sharp chink of metal against metal and the stolid clopping rhythm of the mules' hooves. The sound of voices floated along, casual and unaware. The headman listened carefully. Though he knew the *ladino* language, the sounds were too soft and blurred to make out what was said. But what he really listened for were the more important qualities that would tell him of sudden apprehension, fear or preparation.

Now he could see them.

They ambled along in single file, even though the trail was wide. Their weapons were slung over their shoulders, and their free hands were thumb-hooked into their web belts or holding cigarettes. They wore the flat-topped green hats affected by Cubans. They make my job easy, the headman thought.

The three mules were at the rear of the caravan, each tethered to the one in front. The last man in the file of *ladinos* held the lead shank of the first mule.

The man in the middle of the file was taller than the others. His face streamed with perspiration. This one was not a *ladino*. Although the realization startled the headman, he did not allow it to interfere with his concentration.

The lead man in the file was nearly abreast of him. The precise moment would come as the *ladino* moved one footstep past him. The headman focused his gaze on his target's neck.

Now!

In a single fluid motion the headman leaped into a half crouch behind his target, his right arm swinging in a wide arc,

[14]

first up, then down. The machete bit deeply, almost sound-lessly, through cloth and webbing into the nape of the target's neck. The *ladino* dropped to his knees, then pitched forward, burying his face in the mud of the trail. The headman whirled to face the rest.

The work was done. Five corpses sprawled, two of them kicking futilely at the floor of the jungle. Cigarettes smol-dered in outflung hands. The headman plucked one from dead fingers and inhaled from it slowly. The Indian faces of his comrades awaited his next command.

"It was well," he said in the Quiché dialect. "Now we shall see what riches the *ladinos* have brought to us."

While he stood apart, finishing his victim's cigarette, his men went to work.

The mules were led to one side. Then the band stripped the corpses, rifling each pocket. They did the same with personal baggage.

In short order, neat piles of gear lined the side of the trail. The corpses, bloody and naked, were rolled to the other side. Already clusters of flies swarmed on the gaping wounds.

"That one is not *ladino*," one of the band announced.

"It is as I expected. He is large. And he wore the boots. The others wore the simple shoes," the headman said, as if to explain all.

"He also has the round blue eyes."

The headman went over to the corpse, paler than the others. His tribesman caught the body under its right shoul-der with his toe and rolled it over on its back.

The headman leaned down and stared into the round, lifeless eyes. "What did he carry?"

"Only papers."

"Money?"

"A little currency. No gold."

The headman grunted. "And the others?"

"The same."

It occurred to the headman that he might lose face over

[15]

this. He had predicted that this band was carrying money and supplies to the enemy guerrillas. At the moment things did not look promising.

"Bring me the carrying bag of the blue-eyed man."

One of his men trotted over with a large square canvas case with carrying straps. The headman opened it and removed the items inside, one by one. They were large folded papers with puzzling figures and lines drawn in blue. Though he could read *ladino*, the headman could not make out the words written on any of the papers, except one: CINABRE, S.A. It meant nothing.

"Are they important?" asked one of his men hopefully.

"Perhaps. We will take them to the gringo. He will tell us." He rummaged in the bag, then threw it aside. "Now let us see what the mules carry."

Eagerly, the band unloaded one of the mules and unlaced the heavy canvas pack.

"What is this?" One of the men handed a length of gleaming metal to the headman, who examined it closely. "It's very heavy." It seemed to be a tube, its ends carefully closed with screw-on caps. The headman unscrewed one of the caps. Suddenly the cap came loose and a stream of silvery metal spurted from the end and fell to the ground.

"What is it?" one of the men demanded.

The headman looked inside the now-empty tube. "I don't know," he said. "We shall consult the gringo. He will give us money and ammunition for all of this."

In fact, the headman was uncertain about the value of this mission. Still, he wanted to reassure his men that the work of days was worth more than a few weapons and mules. He hoped the gringo displayed his usual lively interest in strange things and odd bits of information.

After they had dragged the corpses well off the trail and brushed up the ground, the Quichés left. Soon the rain forest was again as it had been. Only a gleaming dot of the silvery liquid marked the place.

II

Mr. Julio Sanchez of Dallas, Texas, would have been shocked at what had transpired in the rain forest earlier that morning, had he known. But even if he had, he would not have related those events in any way to the cable he held in his hand. In fact, the cable's senders did not know about the jungle confrontation either. Not yet.

But there was a common denominator.

Cinabre, S.A.

On the record, Mr. Sanchez was a commercial agent, a middleman, a broker. He had reasonably good papers that established him, and ample funds to support his activities on behalf of certain nebulous foreign interests. He saw to their needs for specialized industrial equipment and materials, technical instruments, and financial transactions. He made a point of not knowing much about his clients once their "credit" was established with him. But he did know the names they employed for business.

Cinabre, S.A., was one of them.

Therefore he had no alternative but to carry out the coded instructions in the cable: "Sell longest possible term futures contracts for delivery of ten thousand kilograms, repeat, ten thousand kilograms, of gold."

My God, Sanchez thought, that's more than ten *tons* of the stuff. Nearly sixty million dollars!

Sweating, he reached for his telephone to start spreading the orders across the world's gold exchanges in Chicago, New York, London, Zurich.

What did Cinabre know? What *could* it know?

PART ONE

Atitlán Volcano

Chapter One

I

Harry Desceau didn't like it.

He didn't like the Russian and he didn't like the Cubans. He especially didn't like their calling him to account. But Harry Desceau had made a career of accommodating people he didn't like, then leaving them with his footprints on their faces.

But business was business. And it was better business to bring the people he didn't like to his own *casa* overlooking Lago Atitlán than for him to go there.

"Okay," he said. "A couple of your men get lost in the bush. It happens out here. Guatemala is a rugged country. Thirty-four rumbling volcanoes and an earthquake every five minutes. Leftist guerrillas, whom you help out, rightist guerrillas other people help out, and Desceau's guerrillas, whom Desceau helps out." He swirled the ice in his tumbler of Scotch. "So what do you want from me?"

The others, holding drinks and cigars, were arranged in chairs and divans around the large, austere room. Desceau hadn't meant it to be austere. But the touches of leather, chrome, and mass-produced abstract prints were remote. The room might have been the lobby of a better Las Vegas motel.

At the same time, whatever there was in the room lost in competition with the incredible lake outside. Its colors changed constantly through the spectrum of blues, greens, and violets as the clouds scudded above it.

Colonel Robert Guiteras studied Desceau.

This, he thought, is a well-packaged thing. Desceau's black hair was slicked straight back. He wore a pencil-thin moustache, a specially tailored vicuña sport jacket, and coordinated flannel slacks. A maroon silk scarf was knotted at his neck and a matching kerchief graced his breast pocket.

This onetime Chicago tough, Guiteras thought, is a dangerous man, even if his muscles have turned to suet. Still, Desceau was a calculated risk. He would be dealt with, then disposed of.

"My group"—Guiteras gestured at the Cubans with him—"is merely interested in getting a status report on Cinabre, S.A." His expression revealed nothing. "It has been more than a year since we embarked upon this project."

"And," interrupted one of the others, "all we have seen are requests for more equipment, more this, more that, now more mercury. But we have nothing to show. *Nada.*"

Desceau crossed the thick beige carpeting to the bar and refilled his tumbler. Then he turned to the vast window looking out on the lake and gestured with his glass toward the mountain on the far side.

"You see it? Atitlán! One of the biggest volcanoes in Central America, right? But it sits there all quiet and nice. Rumbles once in a while, shakes our feet. But it stays nice and quiet, right? And then one day—wham!" Whiskey sloshed from his glass onto the carpeting.

"What is that to us?" Guiteras demanded.

Desceau tapped his chest. "Harry Desceau is like that volcano." He sipped Scotch. "Now, we started this Cinabre corporation, and—as far as you are concerned—nothing is happening. For all you know, what you've sent in to us may have disappeared into the bush like your men and their mules the other day."

Guiteras nodded. "Some of our people are demanding some accountability for this matériel. The aggregate is now in the millions."

Desceau's eyes narrowed. "Maybe there are people in Havana who think I'm stealing their goods instead of following through on the deal."

Guiteras was unintimidated. "The matter became somewhat urgent after the United States District Court in Washington handed down those indictments against you. The confidence of some who otherwise would support this project was shaken."

"They're out to get me," Desceau exploded. "Listen. Do you know who the worst enemy of the American businessman is? You Communists? Wrong! It's the U.S. government." Desceau finished his drink and refilled his glass.

"True or false, these matters *do* raise questions."

"Don't forget one thing," said Desceau. "You came to *me* because you needed me for this job, and you got me. And when I make a deal, I follow through."

"To be sure," said Guiteras. "But my superiors in Havana would like some *small* reassurance, especially after the unfortunate disappearance of the caravan. . . ."

"That was a mistake, I admit that. I was trying a new route and it turned out to be wrong."

"Why a new route?"

Desceau stared into his glass. "For months now we have been moving the goods overland from here. It's a longer, more difficult route, and it costs more, both to pay my own guerrillas for guards and to bribe the other guerrillas to stay out of our way. On the other hand, our floatplane is quick and can land at both ends easily, but it doesn't carry much and it can't handle heavy matériel . . . especially heavy liquids like mercury."

"I understand."

"So we tried a new route straight in from the coast, and . . ." Desceau shrugged.

"This could be dangerous if the caravan was taken by the American-sponsored guerrillas."

"How?" Desceau pressed. "They capture a bunch of

[23]

mercury-filled tubes. What does that mean to them? Nothing."

"But what of Cinabre?" Guiteras asked.

"No problem, Colonel." Desceau waved toward a stocky, bald man who had been sitting on a divan apart from the Cuban delegation. "Doctor, tell them what's going on."

The man stood and took a clipboard from under his arm. "I haven't met all of you before," he said. "I am Dr. Timofey Karuchkin. You may know me by my cover name, George Timothy." He glanced at his clipboard. "The concept for this project occurred to me while I was involved in applied nuclear research in the Soviet Union. I broached the idea to my government. Instead of praise for my initiative, I was reproached. Their attitude was: Why should the world's largest producer of noble metals desire to develop a system that, in effect, would virtually eliminate the *market* value of those minerals. Not the intrinsic value, mind you, but the *market* value." He looked around the room for a response. Seeing none, he went on.

"To me as a scientist, their attitude was distressing. To me as a Communist, their perspectives were heretical. I made up my mind to take steps.

"Happily," he went on, "I was dispatched to Cuba to help supervise the maintenance of the Soviet submarines' nuclear propulsion systems. There I made the acquaintance of Colonel Guiteras." He nodded at the Cuban, who smiled encouragement. "As our friendship developed I saw that there were real opportunities to advance my nuclear concepts in the more progressive Communist environment of Cuba."

"Thank you, Doctor," said Guiteras. "Perhaps you could compress this most interesting history somewhat. . . ."

"Forgive me. Of course." He fumbled with the clipboard. "Subsequently, certain senior Cuban leaders immediately realized the significance of my plan. They accepted and encouraged it. They also recognized the vital need to carry out their work without the knowledge of the Soviet Union or anyone else. As a consequence, three things were required to implement this project.

"First, a quantity of enriched uranium fuel had to be obtained.

"Second, I would have to disappear.

"Third, a secret place far from the prying eyes of the Soviets and their friends would have to be developed to carry out the project and, as it turned out, to secure adequate finances.

"We accomplished these steps, as you know. It took many months, but I was able to extract an inventory of nuclear fuel from the submarine systems." He chuckled. "Even now there are seven vessels limping about the Caribbean wondering, no doubt, what has gone wrong in their propulsion.

"As for me, Colonel Guiteras arranged for my accidental 'drowning.' The body was never recovered, of course. As for the third part . . ."

". . . That's where I come in." Desceau's voice boomed out from behind the bar. "You may hate capitalists, but when you wanted to do the job, you had to turn to one for help. Harry Desceau is the name, and Cinabre is the game."

II

At that moment, two thousand miles due north from Atitlán, in the crumbling northeast quarter of the District of Columbia, others were also curious about the prospects for Cinabre, S.A.

In a paneled room, two men sat facing each other across a broad walnut desk. Behind the desk, drawn gold draperies that matched the carpeting suggested a window, but they concealed only a thick concrete wall.

"So, you've come to the Bank." The old man on the creditor's side of the desk leaned forward in his leather swivel chair. His voice accused.

The younger man shifted in his seat. "Have you heard of Cinabre, S.A.?"

"It sounds like a toothpaste."

The other man smiled in spite of himself. "It's a corporation. In Guatemala."

"And the Bank is a corporation in Washington. What of it?"

It was true, of course. The Bank, in fact, was the venerable and unremarkable Grain Exchange & Merchants Trust, housed, as it had been since the Civil War, in a shabby brick building in one of Washington's decaying neighborhoods. Its threadbare Victorian lobby with the black iron tellers' cages, its tarnished cuspidors and cancerous rubber plants, seemed to contradict the American business spirit.

Actually, the GE&MT handled only very special accounts. It did not seek clients and rebuffed those few eccentrics who sought its services. It was a point of pride with the Bank that no felon ever had been tempted to rob it. Its ownership was obscure, its stock held in a variety of trust and investment organization names. Indeed, it filed all of the myriad government forms that institutionalized its existence. Who cared that the GE&MT's peeling facade abutted a large, nameless and windowless building of modern form? Its books balanced. It turned a profit.

And it reported from time to time to that United States government agency known euphemistically as "the Company."

The younger man was a senior officer of the Company. Despite his rank, however, he deferred to the older man, known to him, and a very few others, as "the Chairman."

"Even if you haven't heard of Cinabre, S.A., you would know the name of Harry Desceau."

"I know it. I read the indictments. They missed the real sewer there."

"The attorneys did what they could."

"What about Desceau?"

[26]

"He's in Guatemala. This Cinabre corporation is his."

The Chairman nodded, but said nothing.

The younger man extracted a file from a large briefcase beside his chair. He thumbed the file, then read. "Desceau, Harry. Forty-eight. Born Chicago. Orphaned. Ran away from foster home at sixteen. Joined marines. Silver Star, Korea. Returned to become a truck-union organizer. Subsequently, became a truck-line operator. Indicted for assault. Acquitted. Indicted for extortion. Acquitted. Named in three murders. No charges. Took control of a truckers' pension fund group . . ."

"Skip it! I know the road. A trail of dirty paper and corpses right up until he took control of International Transit Finance and those offshore funds. He started as a petty crook. and in the good old tradition of free enterprise worked his way up to a big-time crook. And now he's exiled in Guatemala with this—Cinabre, is it?—up to no good. What's that to the Company? And why bring it to the Bank?"

From the file the other man withdrew a printed document and tossed it across the desk.

The Chairman riffled it. "A prospectus for Cinabre, S.A. Desceau is selling stock. And he'll find suckers to buy."

"Look at the statement of purpose."

The Chairman found the place. " 'To engage in the active mining of cinnabar and such other mercury-bearing ore as' . . . mercury?"

"Exactly."

The Chairman was thoughtful. "It's a valuable mineral, of course. A little out of Harry's line, but . . . ?"

The younger man took from the briefcase a length of stainless-steel tube and laid it on the desk. "One of our . . . subsidiaries . . . intercepted this tube and a number like it in a caravan headed *toward* the Cinabre mine site. Each tube was filled with mercury."

"What is it?"

"We have no idea."

[27]

"Is mercury usually carried in such a container?"

"No."

"Did you say they were carrying the mercury *to* the mine?"

"Correct."

"And where is the mine?"

"We've located it on a small lake in a subsidiary chain of the Sierra Madre. Almost inaccessible." He handed the old man a topographic map with the mine location marked.

The Chairman read a designation. "The Sierra de *Flan?*"

"Flan is a kind of custard dessert. . . ."

"I know that! Who the hell named it?"

"That's the actual name. It's kind of a sick joke, really. That's earthquake and volcano country."

"You're sure the mercury wasn't being carried away from the mine?"

"We're certain."

"Odd."

"Odder still when you factor in other bits of information."

"Such as?"

"The Cubans are participating covertly in the project. They've supplied a lot of equipment and matériel. We don't know what. It all went to the mine site. In fact, one of the individuals in the caravan was a Chilean engineer working for the Cubans. The Cinabre board of directors is made up of Cuban agents."

The Chairman nodded. "Ardent Communists engaged in a classic capitalist venture. What did the engineer have to say?"

"He wasn't in a position to say anything. From his manuals and so on—some in Russian, by the way—he was apparently a specialist in electrical energy systems."

The Chairman glanced through the prospectus. "Who is Dr. George Timothy, director of research?"

"We don't know."

"But you've identified the others."

"Correct."

The Chairman grew impatient. "I still see nothing here of special interest to the Bank. The fact that a snake like Desceau has teamed up with the Cubans to run some kind of mercury mine doesn't concern me."

"Until one asks why they were taking mercury *to* the mine? And why these steel tubes?"

"From Desceau's record I would say he is cooking a swindle, salting the claim, perhaps. Who knows? I still see nothing for the Bank."

"There could be," said the younger man. "Suppose you sold Cinabre shares short, then *closed* the mine. . . ."

"We don't undertake such missions on whim," the Chairman growled. "Why doesn't the Company look into the matter directly?"

The younger man winced. "Not long ago we would have. But now there are . . . restraints." He went on in some detail about how his agency had been forced to restrict its active operations in the wake of extreme congressional pressure and public outcry. "As a result, we are slowly turning away some of our longtime clients. Even the intercept that got *this* information"—he gestured at the steel tube—"was outside the bounds."

"They're a bunch of damn fools up on the Hill," the Chairman muttered.

"But the Bank is outside their purview," the younger man suggested.

"Perhaps." The Chairman closed the file and looked up at the other man. "All right. We'll make an inquiry and report. That's all. Unless, of course, there is something there of value to the Bank."

"That's all we ask."

The younger man left the way he had entered, past the tiers of humming electronic equipment, through the alarm system, through the thick oak door, and, finally, back into the musty nineteenth-century lobby of the Grain Exchange & Merchants Trust.

[29]

III

The Chairman wasted no time. Flicking the switch of his intercom, he said, "Check the Firebird Incorporated file. They're operating somewhere in the Caribbean area."

While he waited, he examined the stainless-steel tube the Company man had left behind. The workmanship was better than one would need for a simple steel container. He put the tube down and smoothed the topographic map again.

Moments later a metallic voice issued from his speaker system. "Firebird is undertaking an overt commercial project in the Petén jungle region."

"What kind of overt project?"

"Seismological work for an American oil consortium."

That figured, the Chairman decided. Explosives were generally used for seismic studies in oil exploration. If any organization could make the inner earth echo to explosions, it would be Firebird and its master of pyrotechnics, Hugo Wolfram.

"Where is this Petén jungle?"

"Northern Guatemala, sir."

"I have a cable to dictate. The code address is FIREWOLF. . . ."

Chapter Two

I

The rain forest of El Petén had been hacked, burned, and blasted away to make room for the oil hunters.

At one end of the two-acre open area stood a small drilling rig. Near it, an ornately carved stela uncovered when the forest was gouged aside marked the place where the Maya had beaten back the jungle a thousand years before.

The middle of the area was occupied by a helicopter landing pad and associated gasoline stores. The rest of the space was filled with assorted Quonset huts and stacks of supplies and equipment.

Near the drilling tower a lean, white-haired man sat in a canvas folding chair, hunched over a low table. From an array of gray metal boxes, each with its own miniature console of dials and switches, loops of multicolored insulated wire trailed to the drill site.

The man's narrow, scarred face was set in concentration as he methodically touched metal calipers first to this connection, then to that one, testing the current flow. Finally, he leaned back and removed his gloves. From the pocket of his ash-colored coveralls he tugged a bandanna handkerchief and mopped streams of perspiration from his face. A white tape ironed over the breast pocket of the coveralls read "Wolfram" in stenciled letters. Under it was a vivid insignia, an orange bird with wings outstretched.

A moment later a stocky black man carrying a bullhorn walked over to him. He wore the same kind of ash-gray coveralls and bird insignia. The name over the pocket was "Magraw."

"How does it look?"

"This damn jungle humidity is the problem. But it's ready now."

"Good." The black man's voice, amplified through the bullhorn, crackled across the clearing. "Seismographs ready?"

At opposite sides of the open space, groups of men huddled around equipment looked up, then waved acknowledgment.

"On the mark!"

Wolfram flicked a row of switches to On.

"Five"—the bullhorn boomed—". . . four . . . three . . . two . . . one . . . *fire!*"

Wolfram threw a large red switch.

The matted surface of the clearing jumped slightly. There was no sound except the far-off chatter of monkeys and the cries of birds.

Wolfram turned to Magraw and chuckled. "Anticlimax, isn't it?"

"Not if it worked."

"It worked."

The bullhorn blared again. "Did it register?"

Arms waved at the perimeters of the clearing.

"I guess it worked."

"You can never be sure with new techniques. But if they've got oil strata there, they'll know it." Wolfram stood up. "You see, I've calculated that an extremely fast detonation . . ."

Further words were drowned in the roar of a helicopter's rotors overhead.

Wolfram and Magraw turned to watch the bubble-faced craft settle onto the landing pad. The turbulence from the big blades thrashed the surface, then diminished as the turbines whined down to silence.

The lanky, youthful-looking man behind the controls unhitched his seat belt and climbed out of the cockpit. He wore the same kind of coveralls as the others and a shoulder holster with an automatic pistol. "Kinsey" was stenciled over his pocket.

Wolfram watched thoughtfully as the tall man strode toward them. A strange one, this flier. Though they had shared danger more than once, Wolfram felt he barely knew him. Kinsey's expression now was, as usual, one of faintly puzzled concern.

"Were you able to figure out why the charges were misbehaving?" he asked.

"Humidity was shorting the circuits," Wolfram replied. "The seismologists were taking so long getting their own circuits in order that mine soaked up the atmosphere."

"How much longer will it take?"

"It won't. We fired the shots just before you came in. You brought the beer, I hope."

"I've got the beer. Nicely altitude-iced. We're about through here, then?"

"Yes, unless they want us to play it again."

"Not at Firebird prices, they won't," Magraw chuckled.

They started toward one of the Quonsets, Wolfram leading the way. Inside, an air conditioner hummed futilely against the heat and moisture of El Petén. Each of them popped open a beer.

Kinsey pulled a thick sealed envelope from his coveralls and handed it to Wolfram.

"What's this?"

"It's something from the Bank. I haven't read it. Harada took it on the minesweeper over the midnight signal, then had to stay up a couple of hours to decode it."

Wolfram sat down on his bunk and tore open the envelope. He read the contents carefully, then shrugged and looked up at them.

"What's up?" Magraw asked.

"Nothing exotic. The Bank wants us to check out a mine site belonging to a Guatemala company called Cinabre. According to the message, that crook Desceau is playing footsie with some Cuban agents in a mercury mine."

[33]

"Desceau? Isn't he the guy who had all those indictments handed down against him a few weeks back?" Kinsey asked.

"That's the one," Wolfram murmured, scanning the message again. "They've been after him a long time."

"What's so important about a mercury mine?" Magraw wanted to know.

"They didn't say. Just want us to case it carefully."

"Where is it?"

"Get the map, Kinsey. Let's see."

The flier retrieved a huge rolled topographic map and un-curled it on the cot. Wolfram took the calipers from his pocket and measured the scale. "We're here in the southern region of El Petén. According to the coordinates from the Bank, the mine is . . . here." He twirled the calipers.

Kinsey read over his shoulder. "Sierra de Flan."

"That's a hundred and twenty miles as the chopper flies."

"Rugged country," Magraw observed. "Alternating high-lands and deep valley."

"That means the actual climate and cover around this mine could be anything from rain forest to altiplano," Kinsey added.

Wolfram checked the coordinates. "It looks like the mine site borders on one of these three lakes. . . ." He measured again. "On this small one at the southern end of the string, to be precise."

"What's your plan?"

"We'll check it out. How's your gasoline supply in the chopper?"

"I can refill here."

"Do that. Tomorrow morning you and I will go down and give this place a quick look from the air. Then we'll see what next step suggests itself."

The first lean rays of sunlight dimly illuminated the gloom of the rain forest surrounding the oil camp as Kinsey checked

[34]

the controls of the helicopter. Everything was in order. Wolfram removed his long-lens camera from its waterproof case, checked the film magazine, then slung it biblike across his chest. He also checked the magazine of the automatic pistol in his shoulder holster.

"Ready?"

Wolfram nodded, climbed into the passenger's seat, and hooked his seat belt.

Kinsey started the turbines, and the big rotor began to turn above them. The sounds ricocheted from the buildings of the sleeping camp. After a few minutes of warmup, Kinsey took the craft aloft. Almost immediately the air became cooler, drier. Below, the encampment faded into its shroud of mist.

Their course took them due southwest toward the jagged purple range of the Sierra Madre. For three-quarters of an hour they cruised above the undulating forest sea of El Petén. Kinsey kept their craft only a few hundred feet above the trees and they could readily make out some of the features below.

The canopy seemed to be all of a uniform height—about a hundred and fifty feet—with occasional towering, massive trees thrusting much higher. In the distance a flock of king vultures turned in great spirals around the site of some animal disaster below. Occasionally, clouds of doves and flycatchers swooped skyward, only to settle back into the safety of the treetops.

Soon the terrain began shouldering upward in a series of ever-steeper ridge lines, which would, in turn, give way again to rain forest valleys. The higher reaches were clouded in patches of thick mist. Ghostly forests of giant ferns and gnarled, stunted trees bearded with moss covered the ground below.

Kinsey gestured at the earphones in Wolfram's lap. He put them on to hear the flier's metallic voice.

"We should be coming up on the region soon. That line of peaks ahead ought to be the Sierra de Flan."

[35]

Wolfram took out his binoculars and scanned the jagged terrain for signs of the lakes. Minutes later, he pointed. "There!"

Several miles ahead and to their right they both could make out the glint of a rather large body of water between high, steep ridges.

"That's the northernmost lake," said Kinsey. "It's by far the largest, according to the map."

Wolfram nodded and readied his camera.

Shortly, Kinsey swung down through a pass in the ridge-line and down over the lake surface itself. Some of the surrounding peaks were the perfect cones of volcanoes. Kinsey followed the shoreline. The terrain here was temperate, some five thousand feet. Too high to be jungle, but low enough for scattered groves of low trees, ferns, and patches of high grass.

Wolfram pointed ahead. "There's the lake outlet." The wide lake narrowed there between two steep ridges that formed a gorge.

As the helicopter passed over this area, Wolfram snapped photographs rapidly.

At its southern end, the lake terminated abruptly at a high dam of fallen boulders. A torrent of water flowed over the rim of the dam and cascaded into a chasm several hundred feet below.

Kinsey followed this route through the gorge until it opened out once again upon the second lake, smaller and narrower than the first. This smaller lake also ended in a dam of rock, thicker at the base and shallower than the first.

"The mine site should be straight ahead now," said Wolfram, adjusting the lens on his camera.

As with the first lake, water tumbled over the rim, but instead of falling steeply, it rushed down a steep incline of broken rocks that pounded the water into a white froth.

Farther along, the decline began to level off. The helicopter had followed the path of water down in altitude now by several thousand feet. Once again they were in rain forest terrain modified only slightly by the altitude. The path of water was placid on this stretch, leading them finally out over a small, still lake.

"There it is! On the right!"

Wolfram kept his camera working, recording the heavily reinforced concrete arch of the mine entrance, outbuildings hugging the steep mountainside, and a flat, paved area between the mine and a fifty-foot pier built of concrete and steel. The pier had tram rails that led back into the mine.

As the helicopter flew past, a handful of startled guards leaped to their feet.

"Bring her around again," said Wolfram. "I want some more of these features."

As Kinsey brought the craft around in a steep turn, a star pattern blossomed suddenly at the top of the helicopter's plastic bubble.

"Those nuts are shooting!" Kinsey shouted.

Through his telephoto lens, Wolfram was staring into the muzzles of the guns as they fired. "Get out of range!" he shouted back.

In seconds Kinsey had their craft well up and away.

"Hold it here for a minute," Wolfram said. "They can't reach us with carbines here."

As the craft hovered, Wolfram photographed the activity. More uniformed men raced out from inside the mine. Finally, a crew wrestled a heavy machine gun out and worked frantically to set it up.

"They just made their point," said Wolfram. "Let's go home."

Kinsey put the craft into a steep climb, found a declivity in the ridgeline opposite the mine area, and passed through. Minutes later, as they retraced their route back toward El Petén, he asked, "What do you think?"

"It's one of the most heavily guarded mines I've seen."

"Mysterious?"

"Not overly. This is guerrilla country. No one would have any enterprise out here without guards. Still, that machine gun was a little too formidable. . . ."

[37]

"Were they Guatemalan troops?"

"No. Guerrillas, most likely. That's probably why the Bank has us nosing around."

"What do guerrillas want with a mine?"

"I take it that's what the Bank wants to know, too. Especially a mercury mine. We'll have to come back and find out."

III

An agitated Dr. Karuchkin emerged from the mine just in time to see the Firebird helicopter disappear behind the ridge. Twenty minutes later he was still there when the Cinabre floatplane negotiated the tricky landing pattern through the lines of peaks and skimmed smoothly across the surface of the lake. The pilot throttled back on the big single engine, then taxied over to the pier. Guards quickly made it fast to cleats.

As soon as the propeller quit turning, Harry Desceau climbed out and looked around.

Spotting Karuchkin, he shouted, "Another two hundred pounds of quicksilver."

From inside the aircraft the pilot and guards manhandled heavy flasks of the liquid metal onto the carts.

"Something has happened!" Karuchkin exclaimed.

Desceau clumped down the pier to him. "Nothing wrong inside, I hope."

"No, no, everything is on schedule."

"What, then?"

"An aircraft flew over the lake just a short time ago."

"Aircraft? What kind of aircraft?"

"A helicopter. The guards saw two men inside. One had either a gun or a camera. They couldn't tell."

"Did it have markings? Insignia?"

"You'll have to ask the guards."

Desceau waved one of the guards over. "Did you see the aircraft?" he asked in Spanish.

[38]

"Yes, sir."

"Did it have markings? Numbers? Letters?"

"Only an insignia on the middle part, like this. . . ." He drew a crude version of the Firebird in the dust with his fingers.

"A bird?"

"Yes, sir. A bird with its wings outstretched."

"What color?"

"Orange."

Desceau nodded. "It shouldn't be too hard to find out who operates a chopper with an orange bird painted on it. At least it's not the *federales*. That's not their insignia."

"But we dare not have *any* intruders here," Karuchkin protested. "Our project must continue with maximum security."

"Don't worry, Doctor. You stick to the machinery and let me worry about the security. The aircraft was probably some American oil or mining company scouting around."

"We should have more troops," Karuchkin said emphatically.

"The hell with that!" Desceau snapped. "The number we have is already costing too much. We also have to pay off the others. Besides, we haven't gotten anything out of that stove you have inside the mountain. *Nada*."

"Wrong!" Karuchkin declared triumphantly. "This very morning the first mass product from the 'stove,' as you call it, was deposited in the lake. Not ten minutes before the intruders came in their helicopter."

"How much?"

"Fifty rods . . . and it's only a beginning."

"Fifty rods! Now that's the kind of news I like to hear. That means fifty net kilos of goods, right?"

"Approximately."

Desceau looked out over the lake. "At current prices that's better than thirty thousand dollars." He chuckled to himself. "Very good, Doctor. *Very* good."

Chapter Three

I

Dinner was black tie.

It was one of Wolfram's rituals that they must dine in style before a mission. He never offered an explanation.

"It's a vestige of some wartime commando mystique," Magraw said.

"But more in the tradition of hearty meals for the condemned," Harada suggested. He and Juanita had left the Firebird ship in Puerto Barrios to join the others for this venture.

Harada was a man of middle height and age. His iron-gray hair and dramatically handsome features had enhanced an erstwhile career as a Japanese Kabuki actor. Prior to that, his wartime activities as an officer in the Imperial Japanese Navy had provided him with an exceptional insight into the workings of tides, currents, and other hydrologic phenomena useful to the underwater placement of mines and demolitions.

Juanita, too, was expert in the ways of the waters, but as a diver, not a technician. Gowned as she was this evening in stark black with only a simple gold chain and cross around her neck, her striking profile could have marked her as an aristocrat in some bygone royal Spanish era. In fact, she had survived the worst streets of Havana, Castro's revolution, and had escaped Cuba altogether.

Four days had passed since the visit to the Cinabre site.

The five of them had flown in that afternoon, together with an array of equipment, in the larger of Firebird's two helicopters. They had left the steaming tropics of Puerto Barrios for the cool olive green and purple highlands of Lago Atitlán. The difference in climate and topography was as remarkable as the lake itself.

Kinsey had brought their craft into Panajachel, not far from their hotel overlooking the lake. A relatively new place, built and furnished in the traditional hacienda style of the *ladinos*, it would be their headquarters for the time being.

As usual, Wolfram wouldn't talk shop during dinner. But now, the meal finished and the brandy poured, he set up a screen at one end of their private room and arranged a projector and a tray of slides for the briefing.

"Now," he began, lighting a meduro claro, "to business. Atitlán is a magnificent place. Personally, I like the volcanoes . . . but that's a professional bias."

The others smiled.

"Actually, I chose it because this area is the home away from home of one Harry Desceau. That makes it the headquarters of the Desceau financial empire, including a corporation named Cinabre, S.A." He drew on his cigar and blew a perfect smoke ring toward the ceiling.

"Harry has a little place down the shore here. Twenty-seven rooms. Harry also has a swimming pool to augment the beauty of this lake, eighty miles in circumference and a thousand feet deep. The whole countryside is steaming with volcanic springs, but Harry has an imported sauna." There was another puff of smoke.

"These frivolities don't make much sense, but we can attribute them to conspicuous consumption.

"Fifty miles from here, Harry also has what he calls a 'mercury mine'—Cinabre. That doesn't make much sense, either—considering Harry's nature—but we can't call it conspicuous. In fact, it is very inconspicuous. Hidden, guarded. The Bank wants us to make an appraisal."

[41]

Wolfram put his cigar aside in a tray. With thumb and forefinger he snuffed out the candle nearest him and switched on the projector.

As the others snuffed their candles, a telephoto color transparency of the mine entrance appeared on the screen. The startled faces of armed guards stared straight at them from what seemed to be a distance of only twenty-five or thirty feet.

"Kinsey, can you identify those weapons?"

The flier squinted. "Russian AK-47s."

"Close, but not quite." Wolfram stood and walked to the screen. He pointed to one of the arms with a dessert fork. "Note the obvious metal stampings of the receiver and the compensator on the end of the barrel."

"So?" prompted Magraw.

"This weapon is one of the *new* AKMs. Very similar in design to the AK-47, but the receiver is stamped metal instead of the heavier machined metal. The AK-47 doesn't have a compensator. The point is that the AKM's have only been in the hands of Soviet troops a short time. Only a very few of the Russians' friends have them. They have not been supplied to guerrillas anywhere."

"In other words, these guards are Russians or someone close to them," said Harada.

"Almost certainly Cubans," Wolfram replied. "Some of their other equipment says as much."

"Harry Desceau has teamed up with the Cubans?" Kinsey laughed.

"On the contrary," said Wolfram. "From what we have been able to learn about Cinabre, it looks like the Reds have joined Harry."

Wolfram filled them in on Desceau's corporate front, Cinabre, and its inclusion of Cuban agents.

"So where do the Russians come in?" asked Magraw.

"Perhaps they don't," Wolfram suggested. "This has none of their earmarks, not directly. That's one thing we will try to determine."

[42]

"And what do we do, exactly?" asked Harada.

Wolfram shook his head. "All I know is that we are to look, see, and report. We will tell the Bank what we know, what we think, what we hear."

"Simple enough," said Juanita.

"Not for you, *muchacha*. You've got the hard part."

"Swimming again?"

"Of course."

"Let's hear it," said Kinsey.

"Right."

A blowup of a topographic map appeared on the screen. "This is the general area, showing the three lakes." Wolfram used his fork to indicate the smallest lake at the bottom of the projection. "And that's the mine—or whatever it really is. As you can see from the altitude lines, there are steep ridges and mountains all around. Very high. The lake itself is at a rather low altitude, and most of the cover around the lakeshore is medium rain forest. Good concealment. But of course we can't land our helicopter there. Too much forest and we'd be observed from the mine."

The fork moved up the map. "This middle lake is in easy range, but the altitude isn't that much higher. The forest is too thick for a landing."

The fork moved to the topmost lake, many times larger than the others. "This lake is in high country, at least two thousand feet higher than the mine. A whole different climate. Plenty of trees, but lots of open ground, too. So, that's where we'll establish our campsite."

"What's our cover story, if any?" asked Magraw.

"Everywhere we go—both here and there—we go as Firebird Incorporated. We have Guatemalan government authorization—and the gear—to do seismographic work. So that's our cover." He paused, then added, "Actually Harry or his stooges probably have spotted our helicopter already. All to the good. Let them ask questions." He smiled. "Maybe Harry will try to retain us for Cinabre. Naturally, we won't hint that we're working on the Sierra de Flan."

[43]

"That must be the seismographer's heaven," Harada observed. "A name like Sierra de Flan does not inspire optimism about the enduring qualities of those mountains."

At that moment, a tall goblet fell over and cracked against the silverware. The projector screen rippled. Everyone chuckled, somewhat nervously.

"You won't be there, anyway," said Wolfram, looking at Harada.

"No? Where, then?"

"Disguised. You'll be an Indian nosing around Desceau's digs. Find out, if you can, what his route of supply is to the mine. We know he has an airplane that can land on the lake, but there must be some overland route Cinabre uses to get in heavy equipment, supplies, or whatever they're using up there."

Harada was delighted. "A thespian once again."

"What do you say when some local citizen asks you in Quiché what you're up to?" Magraw asked.

"I'm fluent in Spanish. If I get an Indian question, I'll speak *ladino*. If worse comes to worst, I can always speak Japanese. I'll tell them in *ladino* that I'm from a tribe over the mountains."

"Make sure you don't wear a recognizable Indian outfit." Wolfram cautioned. "They wear their clothes like tribal uniforms here. You don't want to get caught in the wrong suit."

"Good point. I'll watch it."

"Meanwhile," Wolfram went on, "the rest of us will go into camp. Kinsey and Magraw will set up the seismography business at the site. Juanita and I will take the diving gear and work our way down the lake chain." He rapped the map again with his fork. "We'll stay undercover in the forest across from the mine until dark. Then we'll swim over."

Kinsey wasn't sure. "These people are armed and very touchy, Hugo. My guess is that they'll have a sentry system. Perhaps patrols. Especially since we buzzed them the other day."

Wolfram triggered the projector to a longer view of the mine area. "As you can see, they have a spotlight arrangement on the outbuildings, on the pier, and on the mine entrance. Illumination is the best security from their standpoint. As for patrols, we have to consider the possibility. But look at the shoreline. Either rocky, rugged, and steep, or thick with rain forest. Very tough to patrol in the dark."

"They can still have their sentries out."

"We'll be on the lookout."

"Let's see the map again," said Magraw.

Wolfram switched back to it.

"What's the distance from the big lake to the mine?"

"About seven miles."

"That's a tough hike in rugged terrain, especially when you're carrying diving gear."

"We'll take it slow. No hurry."

Wolfram looked around at the faces visible in the light of the projected map. "Any more questions?"

"What about guerrillas?" asked Kinsey.

"It's a minimal risk. We've already identified the dominant armed group in this area. We'll just have to hope they aren't in a feud with some other group."

"One other thing," said Harada. "What do we call these lakes for communication purposes?"

Magraw suggested giving them numbers or letters.

"Good idea." Wolfram rapped his fork on the map. "Alpha is the big lake. Beta is the middle lake. The Cinabre lake is Gamma." He switched off the projector. "We leave in the morning."

II

Harry Desceau met for dinner that night with the "directors" of Cinabre.

Colonel Guiteras lit a cigarette calmly. "We cannot just let this matter slide, Mr. Desceau. It has become a matter of real concern."

Desceau poured Scotch into a tumbler. "The project is on schedule. When the goods are ready, we'll start the pipeline operating. My subsidiaries in the States, in London, and in Europe are ready to go. The equipment is in place. What else do you want?"

Guiteras rubbed his thumb and forefinger together. "Results. When?"

"I told you," Desceau snapped. "The first production is only fresh out of the stove—"

Guiteras interrupted him. "The end of the week?"

"That's what Karuchkin promised."

"We will count on it," Guiteras said without much conviction. "In the meantime, what about the helicopters?"

"Look," said Desceau, "oil exploration is going on all over El Petén. Geologists are knocking around in the highlands, looking for minerals. . . ."

"If these helicopters make themselves obnoxious," said Guiteras, "what can *they* do and what can *we* do?"

"From the air they can do nothing," Desceau replied. "The only danger is they will see us dumping cylinders into the lake once a day."

Guiteras nodded.

"We can move the dumping time to sundown. At dusk we'll still have enough light to see, but aircraft wouldn't be able to see in. We'll switch the lights on later."

"What if the aircraft land?"

"It's not likely during the day. In any case, there is no place for a helicopter to land unless it has floats. The ones we've spotted don't."

"Are there places for a helicopter to land nearby?" asked Guiteras.

"The mountains immediately around us are too rugged."

"Everywhere?"

Desceau thought a moment. "Before we moved into the

old Spanish silver mine, we checked out some possible supply points. There's one seven or eight miles north in the highland country. Good landing spaces, but it's a hard hike down from there, and there's no security. To have set up operations there, we would have had to have a defense perimeter with a company of troops against the guerrillas."

"But the others could land there?"

"Sure."

"Send a squad out to patrol. We cannot take chances," Guiteras warned.

"*Half* a squad," Desceau objected. "We're going to need the rest to unload the mules when the caravan comes in."

"Very well. But the patrolling must begin in the morning."

Chapter Four

I

Part of Wolfram's plan involved planting a well-documented cover story as protection. A coded telegram to Firebird's home office in Houston detailed their fictitious seismographic project in a cipher suited for third-graders. A copy of it would surely reach Desceau.

In their rooms each member of Wolfram's crew had planted in luggage or clothing various bits of information, correspondence, or plans referring to their work. These references could be checked; all of it would verify.

From the evidence any moderately clever analyst would deduce that the Firebird group had been retained by some prominent nickel or copper syndicate to develop data on possible ore sites.

They left their hotel quite early—and quite noisily—that morning, after advising the hotel management that they would return in three days or so. Kinsey complained loudly about the length of the flight, naming an area in a direction other than the one they intended to take.

When they arrived at the helicopter, Harada, his rucksack loaded with his Indian garb, rations, and a revolver, slipped off into the shadows, while the others boarded the flight.

The sun was barely tinting Atitlán volcano when their craft pulled up and away. Kinsey set a temporary course in the false direction, then a few miles away veered back to the true course.

The flight through the jagged mountains was impressive but uneventful. Forty minutes later Kinsey spotted the Alpha lake, glittering gold in the morning sun. After a brief reconnaissance, the flier found an open patch along the shoreline near the southern outfall and settled down.

"What a magnificent place!" Juanita exclaimed as they scrambled out into the brisk highland air. She ran to the water's edge and plunged her hand into the clear water. "Cold, Hugo!" she shouted. "Very cold."

"And it won't be any warmer down below. At sunset a thick mist will form over Gamma lake."

"All the better to hide us."

"But all the more difficult for *us* to see."

"We'll set the tents up under the trees," said Magraw, indicating a nearby copse of gnarled evergreens festooned with moss.

"Very well," Wolfram agreed. "Juanita, you take charge of packing our diving gear and the other equipment."

"We'll need the wet suits for the cold water."

"I'm afraid so." He didn't like the idea of the extra weight.

"Shall I spread the camouflage net over the chopper?" Kinsey asked.

"Don't bother. We're supposed to be here on commercial business. Somebody might wander by and wonder why we're hiding."

The business of setting up the camp went quickly. Twice the ground trembled underfoot, and they could hear the cracking of boulders bounding down a distant slope.

By ten o'clock the tents and the seismographic instruments were set up. Satisfied with appearances, Wolfram called them all over to the helicopter. He held up a hand radio.

"I don't want to use this thing any more than absolutely necessary, but one of you will have to monitor your end all the time."

Kinsey and Magraw nodded.

"I'll signal only if we spot a patrol. The signal will be just a

[49]

digit for the number of personnel, like 'seven' or 'ten' repeated a couple of times. All I need is a 'roger' response. Nothing more. You can assume they're coming your way.

"When we get to the lake, the signal will be 'gamma.' If there's trouble, I'll say whatever I can."

"What do we do about it?" asked Magraw.

"Play it by ear. We'll try to bluff our way out with the cover story."

"How will you explain the diving gear?"

"We're planting underwater sonic devices. I've got some charges of C4 in my kit for . . . problems."

The others looked skeptical.

"I know," Wolfram conceded. "It's lame, but. . . ." He swung his heavy pack of air tanks, nylon rope, and miscellaneous equipment to his shoulders and buckled up.

"I wish we had some rifles," Kinsey muttered.

"Wouldn't do any good," said Wolfram. "They hold all the trumps in a shootout. Bluff is our only weapon."

Kinsey helped Juanita shoulder her pack while Magraw took a machete and hacked a stout hiking staff for each of them.

"We'll be back tomorrow," said Wolfram. Minutes later he and the woman had disappeared through the woodland along the lakeshore.

II

The Cinabre patrol was slow in getting started.

Because of unusually poor radio reception in the mountains, the order had been transmitted via the daily flight to the lake.

Karuchkin gave them their instructions in the absence of Desceau and Guiteras, who had remained at Atitlán.

"Go up to the big lake today, keeping a sharp lookout as you go."

"For what?"

"A helicopter. People. Anything unusual."

"Then what?"

"Report to me for instructions."

"How long shall we stay out?"

"It's important that you be back here before dark tomorrow. We have a caravan coming in tomorrow afternoon or the next morning. We'll need all personnel to help unload and store the material."

"We will camp by the big lake tonight, then return in the morning. That will give us time to rest up for the caravan work."

"Any questions?"

"What if there is shooting?"

"Shoot back, of course. And report."

"Yes, sir."

"Very well, then. Off you go."

It was nearly noon as the officer and his three men began to pick their way northward along the rugged shoreline.

III

After the helicopter had left, Harada changed quickly into his Indian disguise—a kind of two-layered kilt, the bottom layer skirt-length, the top layer, knee-length, of checkered wool. His jacket was a threadbare *ladino* tunic, over which he wore a brightly colored serape. On his head was a Mayan turban of bandanna material. He was confident his garb would enable him to blend effectively into the Indian background.

Following Wolfram's general instructions, he wandered along the lakeshore, passing early-rising villagers carrying huge bundles of kindling, until he reached the outer perimeter of the Desceau compound, a high chain-link fence with a double apron of barbed wire on top. Inside the fence, trees and shrubs obscured all but the roofline of the mansion. No one seemed to be about, but scaling the fence was out of the question.

Instead, he followed it inland. Midway down the fenceline there was a gate flanked by a small guardhouse that was occupied by a sleepy *ladino*.

Harada walked slowly to the shelter. He waited silently by its window until the drowsy guard suddenly became aware of his presence.

"What do you want?" he asked brusquely in Spanish.

"I look for a job."

"There's no work here. Go away."

"A man in the town square said there was work here."

"You Quiché?"

"No."

"Where you from?"

"From far over the seven mountains." Harada waved vaguely at the distant volcanoes.

The guard studied Harada's garb. "What tribe?"

"Nihonango."

"Never heard of them."

There was no reason he should have, Harada thought. The word was a compound of Japanese and the native word for "place."

"You know how to drive mules?"

Harada nodded.

"Well, we have all the mule drivers we need. Go home. When we hire more mule drivers, come back."

Harada turned to go. Mule driver! He nearly laughed aloud at the idea. Where in all Guatemala had he seen any mules? Ox carts, yes; an occasional horse, yes; motor vehicles, yes. But mules?

No.

And yet they were powerful pack animals, well suited to mountain trails. And of course they were especially suited for caravans through all kinds of terrain. Cinabre caravans, perhaps?

[52]

If he found the mules, Harada thought, he would probably find the staging area for Cinabre's supply expeditions into the interior. He might also discover what these caravans transported.

From the Desceau compound Harada hiked the more than six miles back through Panajachel to the larger town of Solola. Rows of Indian vendors lined the streets near the clock tower of the ancient colonial municipal palace, hawking fruits and vegetables, cloth, and artifacts.

"Where do I find the mules?" he asked a fruit vendor. "The what?"

"Very tall horses with long ears." Harada held his palm to his temples to demonstrate. "They make this sound." He hee-hawed loudly.

The fruit vendor described the problem in Quiché for the small crowd that had gathered around them, repeating Harada's descriptive gestures. Harada glanced around nervously for signs of "official" interest. A policeman inside the palace foyer watched for a moment and then turned away.

"Have you seen such creatures?" Harada repeated his question several times.

There was no response from the small crowd.

Harada pulled some silver coins from his jacket pocket and tucked them between the closed fingers of his right hand.

"I look for the horse with the big ears and the loud laugh," he told them. He held up the hand with the coins for them to see. "These animals come, and you see them and then"—he passed his left hand over the coins—"they disappear into the mountains."

The coins were gone from the right hand. The Indians gestured excitedly at his clenched left fist. Slowly, Harada opened the fist and showed them an empty palm.

As the crowd chattered, one old Quiché pressed forward and whispered something to the fruit vendor.

"This man," the vendor told Harada, "says there are such beasts in the town of Atranango."

[53]

"Where is this place?"

"You must go first to Chichicastenango." He pointed north. "A bus travels there to the church of Santo Tomás. Then it is a mountain road to Atranango. You must walk, for there is no bus. The beasts and their masters gather there, so he says."

"I thank you."

Harada leaned forward and seemed to pull one of the coins from the vendor's ear and gave it to him. The crowd buzzed. Then Harada did the same for the old man.

After that, he left to find the bus depot.

Chapter Five

I

Again the grate of rock against rock sounded a warning. Wolfram's fingers clawed into the wet, mossy surface quaking beneath him. He pressed his body against the outcropping of rock and ducked his head. Close by, he heard the clackety-clack of large stones ricocheting down the jagged face of the Alpha dam. The taut nylon line between him and Juanita went slack around his shoulders and the anchor rock.

"You okay?"

"I'm down."

This last thirty-foot drop was the steepest part of the long descent from the highland lake. Quickly Wolfram lowered his pack down the line, then followed, "walking" almost parallel to the ground level below.

Juanita and Wolfram, safely on firm ground again, stared back up into the spectacular rainbow formed in the cascade of cold mist and spray. "These earthquakes," said Juanita. "It makes me want to get away from this dam quickly."

Wolfram nodded. "And that was just a little one." He looked around. Giant ferns huddled on the sparse knobs of soil, leaning outward to catch the sun's rays that filtered through the constant mist. "We'll leave the rope. We'll need it to get back."

The descent had taken them most of the morning. It was now past noon.

"Hungry?" She shook her head. "Let's move on."

"The going should be easier now."

"Until we hit the rain forest." She patted her machete. "Then the hard work begins again."

Wolfram reshouldered his heavy pack and picked up his staff. "We'll stick with the eastern edge of the gorge. That'll bring us up on the side of Gamma lake, opposite the Cinabre site."

The foaming rapids below the cascade gave way to pools and stretches of placid water. About a mile below the Alpha dam they came to the headwaters of Beta lake.

"Time to eat," said Wolfram. "But let's keep out of sight."

Gratefully, Juanita dropped her pack into a copse of ferns. Wolfram dropped his beside hers. While she dug out the rations, he crawled to the lakeside and scanned the opposite shoreline with binoculars. Nothing. He moved the glasses higher up on the ridge behind the lake and scanned again along a line of sparser foliage. A flash caught his eye farther up the slope.

"I think we have company over there."

Juanita crawled up beside him. "A patrol?"

"Don't know." He adjusted the glasses slightly, then picked up four figures emerging from behind a wall of evergreens into his field of vision. "Nuts!"

Juanita pressed a ration can and spoon into his hand. "What is it?"

"Take a look."

She peered through the glasses while he spooned down some of his ration. "Four men carrying guns," she said.

"They're carrying AKMs, to be precise. Those are some of the boys from Cinabre."

"Do you think they know anything about our camp?"

"Not unless they have a sentry post up there someplace. But I'd say they're planning a long hike that way."

"How can you tell?"

"They're carrying backpacks. That means blankets, rations, gear for at least two days. Plenty of time to get up to Alpha lake and spot our chopper."

"We'd better warn the others."

Wolfram scrambled back and got his hand radio. Pulling out the antenna, he said into the speaker, "Four." A moment later he repeated it. But the response band barely crackled.

"No answer?" Juanita asked.

Wolfram examined the radio. "Might have gotten wet." He snapped the back panel off and examined the insides. "All dry."

Again he took the binoculars and studied the patrol stumbling along the steep slope. Above them the mountains soared into pillows of white clouds. Wolfram pushed the ferns aside and looked eastward toward another towering set of mountain peaks.

"The terrain may be blocking our transmission." He stood. "Wait here. I'm going up the slope a little way to see if more elevation will help."

With his machete he marked a trail from the lakeside back toward the eastern ridge. Moments later he broke out of the thicker jungle foliage into the less luxuriant evergreens of the higher level.

Once again he studied the far-off Cinabre patrol. They were resting in the shade of some low trees, eating their rations, smoking. He put the glasses aside and pulled out the radio antenna.

"Four . . . four." He pivoted around, hoping to catch a radio echo. "Four . . . *four*!"

The static continued. Then came a barely audible "Roger."

Wolfram sighed and retraced his path back down to the lakeside.

"You reached them?"

"Yes, but our signal from Gamma lake is going to be totally blotted, I'm afraid. We'll be farther away and lower down inside the mountains."

"Do we continue?"

"Of course."

[57]

II

The rickety bus from Solola to Chichicastenango made good time, considering its burden of Indians, baggage, bundles, and chickens. After the crossing stop at the Inter-American Highway, Harada elected to ride the last eleven miles clinging to the vehicle's empty door frame. It offered the only possible jump to safety on the twisting road.

The disaster he anticipated, however, didn't occur. The cargo of people, goods, and animals arrived in varying degrees of health in front of Santo Tomás church by mid-afternoon. Harada retrieved his shoulder bag, then approached one of the Indians squatting on the steps of the ancient Dominican structure.

"What is the way to Atranango?"

"Difficult, but not unpleasant," the Indian replied in heavily accented Spanish.

"What trail do I follow?"

The Indian thought about it. Finally, he said, "I don't know."

Harada smiled in spite of himself, then looked around for someone else to ask. Parked on the opposite side of the plaza was a six-wheeled truck. Vintage U.S. Army, thought Harada. He worked his way around the square to the truck and looked it over. It was unmarked and apparently unattended. A coat of bright blue paint covered the original olive drab.

Harada walked around to the back and tried to peer over the closed tailgate. It was too high. He grasped the upper lip of the gate and pulled himself up. At that moment hands grabbed him roughly from behind, pulled him down, and spun him around. An angry *ladino* slapped Harada hard on the jaw and snapped something in Quiché.

"I don't know that language," Harada sputtered in Spanish. "I'm a stranger."

"You were looking for something to steal."

"No, no. A man—over there—said there is need for a

mule driver in Atranango. He said this truck goes there."

"The need for mule drivers is gone."

"Gone? Something has happened to the mules?"

The man laughed. "Yes. Something happened to the mules. They left this morning."

Harada feigned stupidity. "They died?"

"No, you fool. They went on a caravan over the mountains."

"Ahhh. A caravan. And what did they carry?"

The man's eyes narrowed. "You ask a lot of questions."

"I need work. Asking questions about the mules will lead me to them. When I am with the mules, I work."

"You have money?"

"Some coins."

"Let me see."

Harada showed him a handful of Mexican and Guatemalan coins. The driver took them. "You can ride with me to Atranango. In the back. I leave now. But touch nothing, you understand?"

"I understand. Thank you."

Harada turned and threw his shoulder bag into the back of the truck, then climbed up over the tailgate with feigned awkwardness. Clutching the gate with his hands, he grinned down foolishly at the driver, who spat at the ground in disgust, then went around to the closed cab and climbed in. A moment later the truck's engine coughed and roared into life in a great cloud of blue exhaust.

As the truck lurched away, Harada examined the cargo around him. He counted twenty metal containers, each marked "Hg—76 lbs." There were a great many cane-length stainless-steel tubes, strapped together in batches of twenty. Each tube was threaded at both ends. In crates there were caps that fitted the rods.

And there was a locked wooden trunk.

That could be something, Harada thought. He glanced at the rear window of the cab, momentarily catching the driver's eyes. If he kept low he would be out of the man's line of sight.

As soon as the truck had left the little town, the roadway became extremely rough. Harada struggled to keep from being hurled against the sides of the truck as he edged toward the wooden chest.

The lock was sturdy, but the hasp was merely nailed to the wood. He worked on of the stainless-steel rods out of its bundle. Using it as a lever, he jimmied the hasp up, then slowly worked the nails loose. He would have to replace them.

With the hasp off, he raised the lid. The chest was filled with printed material, what appeared to be texts, monographs, and mathematical tables—all in the Cyrillic alphabet. What would Desceau, an American, and his Cuban cohorts want with a lot of Russian texts?

Harada's Russian was weak, but the printed equations and graphs suggested that these books were advanced scientific documents of some kind. A proper translation might tell them all they would need to know about the Cinabre operations.

Quickly, Harada stuffed three of the more technical-looking monographs into his shoulder bag, closed the chest, and replaced the nails carefully. Holding onto the steel tube, he crawled to the back of the bouncing truck.

As it slowed to a crawl at a particularly sharp curve, Harada vaulted over the tailgate and began the trek back to Chichicastenango.

III

Kinsey removed the radio earphones.

"Here they come," he shouted from the helicopter at Magraw, who was dozing beside one of the seismographic sets.

The Cinabre patrol, which had finally appeared at the Alpha lake outfall, could hardly miss the big Firebird helicopter.

Magraw came over to the helicopter. "I guess we'd better go into our act."

"Look scientific."

They settled themselves into folding chairs in front of the seismographic equipment clusters, as if each were monitoring a set of graphs rolling out of the machines.

"According to my chart there have been six earthquakes of measurable energy since we've been here," said Magraw.

"Only six? How can you tell from those chicken tracks?"

"You're fired."

Kinsey laughed. "I only hope our visitors aren't a visiting delegation of Cuban earthquake wizards."

They both concentrated on the equipment. Five minutes later, two members of the patrol emerged through the trees and approached.

Magraw pretended to be startled. "Where did you come from?" he asked in English.

"Do you speak Spanish?" one of them asked.

"*Si.*"

"I am Lieutenant Negrón of the Cinabre Corporation security force."

"How do you do? I am Mr. Magraw and this is Mr. Kinsey. We are with the Firebird organization."

"Firebird?"

Magraw took a business card from his pocket and pointed at the orange bird insignia, then at the large one on the helicopter. "Firebird."

"What is your business here?" Negrón asked evenly.

Magraw waved at the equipment in front of him. "Seismographic studies."

"What for?"

"The tremors tell us a lot about what the rocks are like under the earth. Certain patterns tell us what kind of . . . minerals we might find there if we dig."

"Indeed." Negrón turned and called out. The other two members of the patrol came out of the woods.

"Looks like you expect trouble," said Magraw, pointing at the Cinabre automatic rifles.

"There are guerrillas and bandits in these mountains. Are you not armed?"

"No. We have no quarrel with anyone. Besides, the government said things were quiet."

"They lie," Negrón said matter-of-factly. "Are you staying long?"

"Until tomorrow."

"Then we must protect you tonight."

"We'll be all right."

"But I insist." He smiled. "I will just notify my base where we are." He unslung his radio and spoke into it. "Cinabre . . . Cinabre . . . come in, Cinabre." He shook the radio, then tried again.

"No answer?" asked Kinsey.

Negrón cursed the radio and slung it back over his shoulder. "The mountains block communications."

"Yes, we had trouble contacting our own people."

"There are more of you?"

"Of course," said Magraw. He pointed across the big lake. "They are over there somewhere."

"When do they return?"

"Tomorrow afternoon," Magraw lied.

Negrón looked troubled. "I must report to my base somehow."

"Why not send a man?" Magraw suggested. Two against three were better odds if need be, he thought. Negrón seemed reluctant. He snapped an order to one of his men, who came forward.

"Security has been a major problem here in the mountains," Negrón told the Firebird pair. "How do I know you are not aiding the guerrillas?"

Kinsey frowned and turned to Magraw. "I think we ought to show the gentleman our papers," he said gravely. "They prove who we are."

"I hate to do that," said Magraw. "That's company business, and this man represents another corporation."

"You have very little choice," said Negrón, putting a hand on his AKM.

[62]

"I see," Magraw growled. He strode over to the helicopter and brought back a briefcase of documents. "Here they are. But they are confidential. I must warn you that I will report this to my superiors."

"Please forgive my rudeness," Negrón said, opening the case. "But all rules are changed up here in the mountains. I must confirm this material with my superiors."

"You intend to steal our papers?"

"Please," said Negrón. "I must insist. They shall be returned to you."

"This is most irregular."

"It is unavoidable." Negrón smiled apologetically and handed the briefcase to the waiting security guard. "Take this to Dr. . . Timothy. Tell him our radio transmission is out and we are awaiting his instructions."

The sun was setting as the runner departed.

Chapter Six

I

Although the sky above the ridge of peaks was still orange in the late afternoon sun, it was already twilight in the gloomy jungle around Gamma lake.

Wolfram and Juanita had settled into a palm thicket directly across from the Cinabre site, a quarter of a mile or more away. Through his binoculars, Wolfram observed three guards slouched near the mine opening, talking and smoking, their AKMs slung from their shoulders, barrels down.

"I wonder how many of them there are," said Juanita.

"We saw four on the mountain. Three there by the mine."

"There's a bunker at the south end of the lake."

"I saw it. There are three or four men there with a machine gun."

"There must be someone inside," she said. "Somebody must be doing the mining."

"If it's a mine."

"There would be at least as many inside as outside, wouldn't there?"

"Probably. I'd say there are a dozen on duty, perhaps an equal number asleep, or at ease inside, waiting for their shift."

"I haven't seen a single person dressed as a miner. No one with a light on his hat. Nothing."

Wolfram nodded. "It is odd. This place doesn't have the look of a mine. It's too clean. No tailings, no debris."

She rubbed her hand across her face. "The water will feel good."

The air was dank, hot, and oppressively humid. Perspiration streamed from both of them. The darkness seemed to enclose the jungle in a still thicker heat. Fingers of mist were drifting up from the colder water of the lake.

"We'll suit up now," said Wolfram. "In another twenty minutes it'll be pitch-dark. Then we go."

"What's the target?"

"When we get across, you'll stay underwater. Inspect the pier. I want to know everything about it. Look at the footings, look for intake and outlet pipes. Is the water coming out hot? How big is the pipe? Be sure you have your compass. The navigation might be tricky getting back here."

"What will you be doing?"

"I'm going in close to the shoreline to take a look at the buildings, figure out what kind of a generator system they have."

"What about the spotlights?"

"I'm counting on the mist. It'll reflect the light like a mirror. But from my side the lights will illuminate my targets."

She looked across the lake at the mouth of the mine, now only a black socket in the face of the graying ridge. "Cinabre. What do you think—"

Her question was cut off by the sudden blast of an air horn at the mine entrance. The honking continued in a steady rhythm. The trio of guards came alert and began running down the narrow paved area paralleling the lakefront toward the bunker.

"What is happening?" Juanita whispered.

"Watch. . . ."

At that moment two robot-like figures waddled from the entrance, each tugging at a long cable, each shrouded in thick silver-colored garments, gloves, and boots. The heads were encased in helmets with reflective glass faceplates.

[65]

"Protective clothing," said Wolfram. "It's like the outfits steelworkers wear when they work near the furnaces."

"But why here?"

Wolfram shook his head and refocused his binoculars for a closer look.

The awkward figures wobbled away from the entrance and down the shoreline, hauling the cables. Suddenly, a heavy tram, painted bright yellow, emerged from the mine entrance and rolled stolidly at the end of the cables, following the narrow-gauge tracks leading to the end of the pier. The shrouded figures were at least a hundred feet away from the cart.

The tracks down the pier were on a slight downgrade. Once past the entrance, the tram rolled under its own momentum. Presently, the figures dropped the tethers. As the tram approached the end of the pier, a hook concealed in the decking flew up and engaged the front axle, at the same time tripping open the front end of the car.

A dozen or so gleaming metal rods tumbled out of the tram and splashed noisily into the lake.

The lumbering figures retrieved their cables and hauled the tram back up the pier, then put their shoulders against it and pushed it back into the mine.

"Interesting," Juanita remarked. "They pull the cart out with their long lines, but they push it back into the mine with their shoulders. Those rods must be very hot. What do you suppose they are, Hugo?"

"I don't have the faintest idea."

"Waste material?"

"It certainly wasn't mine wastes. Not in that form. In fact, that stuff didn't look like waste at all." Wolfram rubbed his chin thoughtfully. "When you're under the pier, see if you can retrieve one of those rods."

Spotlights suddenly illuminated the mountainside across the lake. Instinctively, Juanita and Wolfram ducked back into the foliage.

"At least that gives us some light to help us get suited up," Juanita said.

A small group of men, one of them wearing a white laboratory coat, walked casually from the mine entrance out onto the pier.

"My camera. Quick!"

Juanita extricated the camera, equipped with a 200-millimeter lens, from her pack and brought it to Wolfram. "Is there enough light for pictures?"

"When they get out on the pier, yes. I've got very fast film in this thing."

Working rapidly, Wolfram shot frame after frame of the group. All of them except the man in the laboratory coat appeared to be Cubans. Wolfram concentrated on the white-jacketed figure. The face was broad, the head nearly bald, the nose wide and prominent. If he was Cuban, he certainly was not typical. More likely he was a North American, a German, a Finn, or—a Russian.

The figures were gesturing at the water, talking rapidly.

"All right," Wolfram said. "Let's suit up and find out what they're all talking about."

II

The Cinabre patrols that ventured as far as the high lake always used the trail on the western ridge, and the courier cursed his own foolishness for trying this shortcut down the steeper eastern side. It was a good thing he had found the rope dangling over that outcropping. He wondered briefly who might have put it there, then hurried on, fearing the growing darkness.

With the Firebird briefcase in one hand, his AKM slung over his shoulder, and a lantern in his other hand, he began to pick his way along the rocky streambed. As he approached the middle lake, the lantern's light began to fade. If the light died, he would have to spend the night in the open jungle, a prospect that frankly terrified him.

He moved along the lake's edge, jumping from rock to rock, stumbling in the pale light of his lantern, wading in knee-deep water. No point in pushing it, he thought. Instead, he would find a large flat boulder and bed down.

On a nearby shelf of rock, he unrolled his bedding and spread it out. The stone was still warm from the sun. He climbed up on it and stretched out, his rifle close at hand, the briefcase for a pillow.

Ten minutes later, he was asleep.

III

Like phantoms, the two sleek black figures groped their way through the foliage and the low-lying mists and slipped quietly into the lake. After the stifling jungle the cold water was refreshing.

Juanita swam easily toward the barely visible glow of one of the pier spotlights. Around her waist she wore a lightly weighted belt, a kit of tools, an underwater lamp with a red filter, and a sack to carry back anything of interest.

She covered the quarter-mile distance quickly. At the pier she pulled herself through a maze of steel-and-wood uprights and surfaced. Looking up through the mist, she could see the solid outline of the pier deck. She paused to listen. There was no sound except the far-off, muffled thud of an engine running.

She went below again to begin her inspection in the veiled light of the surface. The structure was made of steel, a bridgelike arrangement of I-beams and angle irons, obviously designed to bear heavy weight.

As she descended, she switched on the red lantern. The mist above would mirror the spotlights and hide anything below.

About ten feet down, she found a thick steel pipe, its end

housed in some kind of a metal box—a filter, perhaps. Putting her hand against it, she felt inward pressure. It was probably an intake pipe for the operations inside the mine.

She worked her way to the end of the pier. The steel rods would be below somewhere, possibly hundreds of feet down. Slowly, she pulled herself hand over hand into the depths. Twenty feet. Thirty. Forty.

If she spent too much longer at these depths, she'd have to worry about the time-consuming problems of decompression.

At fifty feet she paused. Below her, strips of metal reflected the red light from her lamp. The rods, all jumbled together, were caught in a wide, deep basket of heavy steel. The basket was linked to cables that fed into the pier, then upward. Apparently this was a lift system of some kind to haul the basket up.

She swam closer.

Around some of the rods the water glowed with a faint blue incandescence. They're still hot, she thought. Even the cold lake had not cooled them yet.

She studied the jumble thoughtfully. There were several rods to one side of the basket that had none of the glow, and she decided to take one of them.

Quickly, she kicked down and grabbed one of the gleaming lengths of pipe. It was unusually heavy, much heavier than she thought a steel rod that size would be. She dropped the rod into her sack and, to offset the added weight, unhooked her lead belt and let it sink into the depths below. Then, clutching a piling, she pulled herself back up to just below the water's surface. Carefully, she emerged again and listened. Still no sound except the engine.

She pushed away into the mist to begin the swim back.

IV

Wolfram was back ahead of her. He put his red lamp in the water as a beacon, then peeled off his tanks and diving suit. The jungle was like a sauna after the lake. Even before he was fully dressed again, perspiration began to stream from him.

He sat down to wait in the darkness. A few minutes later, he heard the splash and slap of Juanita coming ashore.

"Hugo?"

"Over here."

"Thanks for leaving the light out."

"Bring it over here. We can use it to pack up."

"Won't they see it?"

"Not through the mist and foliage. Did you get some rods?"

"One. They're very heavy."

"Oh?"

"Some of them were still glowing hot."

"After all that time in the lake? Let me see what you got."

He carefully inspected the rod she handed him. "Just like the ones the Bank described." He hefted it. "About ten pounds."

"What's it for?"

"We don't know. Apparently, it's filled with mercury. See those caps?"

"Can we open it?"

"We'd better let it alone. The government people will want it in one piece."

"How was your trip?"

Wolfram shook his head. "Couldn't see a damn thing."

"Let's get back to the others. Do you think the Cinabre patrol located the others?"

"We have to plan that they did. That's why we ought to get back before daylight if we can." He stood up. "You pack the gear. I'll sink the air tanks in the lake. We'll save that much weight, anyway. Put the rod in my pack."

In moments they were on their way.

Chapter Seven

I

The courier awoke quite suddenly from his nightmare, his arms and legs pinioned, his face covered.

"Argh!" he shouted, trying to twist loose. His voice was muffled, he could hardly breathe.

"Easy, easy." The woman's voice had a trace of Havana accent.

He was fully awake now, gasping; cold sweat beaded his face.

"We won't hurt you."

"Who?"

"We have some questions."

"Free me at once." The demand sounded ludicrous, even to him.

"You want to drown in the lake?"

He grunted a negative.

"Where did you get the briefcase?"

"From the men at the helicopter."

"Where are you taking it?"

"To Cinabre." He twisted. It was no use.

"Where is the rest of your patrol?"

"At the helicopter. By the big lake."

"Who ordered this to happen?"

"Cinabre."

The courier felt hands fumble with his belt and remove it. An instant later it was pulled tight around his arms, which were pinned under the blanket. Other hands roughly yanked his wrists behind him and tied them. His ankles got the same treatment.

"You're leaving me like a pig staked out for a jaguar," he protested. But there was no answer.

II

The black mass of the eastern mountains seemed to cut into the slowly brightening sky. The predawn air was still, clear, and cold. Over the lake, mist hovered above the smooth water.

Kinsey got up stiffly and stretched, hugged his blanket around his shoulders, and stamped his feet against the chill. The Cinabre guard by the helicopter was suddenly alert. "Stand still," he told Kinsey quietly. The flier obliged.

The others were asleep, huddled in their blankets near the dead ashes of last night's fire. Kinsey scanned the camp, then turned back to the guard. "When does the courier return?"

The guard shrugged and put his finger to his lips. Kinsey glared at him for a moment, to no effect. He looked around again, wondering how Juanita and Wolfram had fared. . . .

What was that?

There it was again—a blink of red near the lake. The sun's reflection? Impossible, not yet.

Kinsey glanced at the guard, who was watching him. But the guard's back was toward the lake and the light. Was it a signal?

He moved his arms up and down under the blanket as if warming himself, a signal of his own of sorts.

The flicker of light came again.

He moved his arms again.

Another wink.

Kinsey's movements seemed to make the guard nervous,

so the flier relaxed. No point in calling any more attention to himself or them, or stirring up the camp. He knew that Wolfram had counted the members of the patrol. But did his colleague know that one of them was gone—one who could return at any moment, perhaps with reinforcements?

He'd have to wait for the answers.

III

Juanita adjusted the binoculars. "He's seen us!" she whispered to Wolfram. "What do we do now?"

"I'm going to work my way up behind the helicopter."

"Make sure Kinsey sees you. He'll distract the guard somehow."

"I'm not worried about the guard. It's the others." He pulled back the bolt of the AKM they had taken from the courier, chambered a cartridge, and switched on the safety. The rifle didn't have the feel of the AK-47. It was lighter. The balance was poor.

"Keep the helicopter between you and the blankets," she cautioned.

"*Claro.*" He patted her on the shoulder. "Don't forget, if things go wrong, get out. Run." He slipped away into the foliage.

As he moved quickly from tree to shrub, he paused often to study his objective. The scene was brightening steadily. The helicopter stood in clear view close by the lakefront. The dead campfires and the blanketed figures of two members of the Cinabre patrol, still asleep, were about fifty yards back toward the woods. The tents and equipment were behind them.

Soon he was between the lake and the helicopter. The big aircraft provided good cover against the guard on the other side and the sleeping men, but no concealment. In fact, he was rather at a disadvantage; the brightening lake behind him would act as a backdrop against which his feet could be silhouetted as he approached. Moreover, his antagonists were well camouflaged against the forest and mountain.

But there was no time for tactical assessments. He would have to trade cover for concealment.

He closed on the helicopter. Under its fuselage he could see the feet of the guard. Slinging the AKM, he went down on all fours. He was certain Kinsey was watching him, for the flier kept moving his arms in awkward gestures, a kind of "all's well." The movements would also hold the eye of the guard.

As Wolfram scrambled under the aircraft, Kinsey shifted his position to a crouch, ready to sprint the twenty feet that lay between himself and the guard.

Carefully, Wolfram brought his rifle around to the ready, switched off the safety, and laid it on the ground next to him. Then, slowly, he reached with both hands for the guard's ankles.

The man shifted from foot to foot. Now he was leaning against the fuselage, with most of his weight on his left foot.

Wolfram pictured how the man would hold his weapon. The right hand would rest on the pistol grip. The barrel would be cradled over the left elbow, pointing toward Kinsey. The safety would be on—or should be. But one couldn't count on that. A shot could fly. The important thing was that it not hit Kinsey.

Wolfram braced himself to clutch the left leg hardest. He struck!

Clutching around the ankles of the guard, he pulled back and up.

The guard thudded to the ground on top of his rifle. Wolfram pulled himself over the prone body and, with the edge of his hand, hammered against the back of the guard's neck.

As Kinsey dashed forward, Wolfram grasped the AKM and brought it up. BU-BU-BUP!

He let fly with a burst of fire over the heads of the suddenly awakened sleepers.

[74]

"Hands up!" Wolfram shouted in Spanish.

Magraw, wide-awake instantly, was on his feet in a split-second.

"What is the meaning of this?" the patrol leader demanded.

"On your feet," said Wolfram. "Move away from those rifles."

"This is outrageous. How dare you fire shots at us."

"Not *at* you, *señor.*"

"I demand an explanation."

Magraw moved around to pick up their rifles. "You are no longer in a position to demand explanations," he said.

Moments later, Juanita appeared. The expression of alarm on her face, once she had sized up the situation, changed into a wide grin.

Wolfram returned her wave and then gestured toward the helicopter. "Kinsey, warm the bird up. We're going home."

The pilot climbed into the craft. In a moment the turbines whined into life and the big rotors began to turn.

"*Señor,*" Wolfram told the patrol leader, "I intend to file a protest with the management of your company. My group came up here on peaceful, private business and with government authorization. So, we will leave the way we came. But I want you to go back and tell your Cinabre, or whatever it is, that they had better not interfere again with Firebird or we will come with our own armed men. And, I assure you, they will be far more adept than you and your band of amateurs."

The Cuban glowered but said nothing.

"Ready when you are, Hugo," Kinsey shouted from the helicopter.

"Let's gather up the gear," said Wolfram. "Don't worry about the packing."

While the others packed up and stowed the camp and seismographic gear aboard the aircraft, Wolfram disassembled all but one of the AKMs and scattered their ammunition. Then, with Magraw's help, he dragged the unconscious

[75]

guard out from under the helicopter and over to his companions. Addressing the patrol leader again, Wolfram said, "I must remind you, *señor*, that I could easily have killed you, then put your bodies in the lake. Your people would never have known what happened to you. I doubt they would really care. But we are not killers, we are business people."

The other man muttered something unintelligible under his breath as Wolfram turned toward the helicopter. He paused before he boarded. "By the way, your courier is tied up in a blanket on the eastern side of the middle lake. On top of a large rock. You can't miss him."

Magraw gave him a hand up, and seconds later, the craft rose out of the campsite. Over the lake, Wolfram pitched the last AKM into the water below.

IV

Later that morning, over breakfast at their hotel on the Lago Atitlán, Harada filled the others in on his adventures as a wandering Indian. He had rendezvoused with them from his hideout in the coffee shrubs as the helicopter returned to Panajachel.

Their rooms at the hotel had been searched, much to Wolfram's satisfaction. Nothing had been taken, but the information gleaned by the searchers, together with the events earlier that morning, would put a tight cover on their operations.

"It's one of the reasons we shun firearms in our projects," Wolfram remarked. "Nothing will punch a hole in a good cover quicker than a bullet."

"Will you leave for Washington right away, Hugo?" asked Harada.

Wolfram patted the heavy suitcase next to his chair. "Packed and ready with what the Bank wants."

"You should get some sleep first," said Juanita.

"I can sleep on the flight north." He glanced at his watch.

"I have to get going. The Washington flight is at twelve fifty."

"What was the printed material, Hugo?"

"I can read Russian, but that might as well have been in Swahili. Very, very technical."

"Subject?"

"Physics, I think. The technicians might make some sense out of it. One thing I know, though. At least one of those documents came from a highly classified file."

Magraw frowned. "High technology at a mercury mine? Whatever for?"

"That's what the Bank will have to tell us."

V

Two hours later, Harry Desceau got word of the Cinabre patrol's embarrassing encounter with Firebird. Colonel Guiteras relayed the message.

"What happened, Colonel?"

"I do not have the full report yet," Guiteras said stiffly. "What were you able to find out about this Firebird organization?"

"It's a technical demolitions company. They put out oil-well fires, make underground tests with explosives—that sort of thing."

"I assume you checked and double-checked everything."

"You assume correctly." Desceau shook his head slowly. "Firebird is so clean it bothers me."

"Why?"

"I don't believe in germ-free companies. And there's another thing that bothers me."

"What's that?"

"The way they handled your patrol last night and this morning."

Guiteras bristled. "My men were unpardonably offguard. I admit that. It will not happen again."

"No, no," Desceau muttered. "I'm not talking about *your*

[77]

men. I'm talking about those Firebird people. They sound just a bit too smooth, too sharp." He stared at Guiteras. "You know, it's amateurs that go in with the guns blazing. It's pros who clean up an operation that quickly, that quietly."

"What do you intend to do?"

"I'll take care of it, Colonel. Don't you worry."

PART TWO

A Matter of Transmutation

Chapter Eight

I

The room, a windowless white box tucked inside one of Washington's newest high-rise buildings, had gray carpeting, a low dais backed by a projection screen, a rostrum, and a table, on which two stainless-steel cylinders and a brown paper bag rested. At the back of the room was a single entry door. The wall was studded with projection eyes. There were ten chairs.

When Wolfram entered at the appointed hour, nine others were there. Except for the Chairman of the Bank, Wolfram knew none of them.

One of the group, a tall man, acknowledged Wolfram's entrance and moved to the rostrum. "Let's get started." He picked up a projection control and ordered the lights switched off. An instant later, the face of Harry Desceau appeared on the screen.

"Our account begins with this man, familiar to anyone who reads the newspapers as a businessman and war hero, philanthropist and swindler, millionaire and corrupter of politicians.

"As you know, he is a fugitive from a number of indictments centering on his political and financial activities. He has managed to evade extradition from Guatemala.

"Actually," he went on, "we had little direct interest in Mr. Desceau until he became associated with this individual . . ."

Another face flashed onto the screen. Wolfram recognized it as one he had seen at the hotel in Panajachel.

". . . Colonel Roberto Guiteras. A Cuban. Background in military engineering. We've had his name for a long time. He was associated with a number of ventures in which we had an interest, not the least of them missile sites constructed in Cuba in the early sixties—and the new, concealed ones built more recently . . ."

A series of pictures flashed on, then off, the screen—high-altitude aircraft, infrared, and satellite photos.

". . . and the new Soviet nuclear submarine facilities. . . ."

Photos of those appeared and disappeared.

"In short, the colonel is noted for his capability in directing complex construction under rather adverse conditions. Consequently, when this individual—using a cover name and story—teamed up with Mr. Desceau in a purported mercury mining venture, our curiosity was piqued. Why Desceau? Why a mercury mine?"

The screen reflected Wolfram's aerial picture of the Cinabre site.

"The answer to the first question appeared simple," the tall man continued. "The Cubans chose Desceau because he would play ball, and—despite his personal legal problems—his financial ventures, companies, and so on, are still intact, providing excellent access to our domestic markets."

He paused before moving toward the screen.

"Our first reading on Cinabre was that the Cubans had concocted a clever ruse to circumvent the strict American embargo against them by entering the U.S. market via Desceau. They need the dollars badly.

"Then some of our . . . surrogates . . . active in Guatemala happened to intercept a shipment of mercury—not *from*, but *to*, the Cinabre site. It became apparent that this mercury venture might be something else altogether. But what?"

The tall man's description of the Firebird probe into the Sierra de Flan was illustrated via scenes familiar to Wolfram—aerial pictures, his own map of the three lakes, and, finally, a photograph of a figure in a white coat.

"Some of you may recognize this man. He is listed in the Cinabre corporate prospectus as a Dr. Timothy, director of research. In fact, he is Dr. Timofey Karuchkin, a Soviet nuclear reactor specialist reported missing and presumed drowned several years ago in Cuba. His mission there was to supervise the repair, quality control, and fuel replenishment for the Soviet nuclear craft operating in the Caribbean. Obviously, this post gave him access to both equipment and fuel for reactors.

"The anomaly here is that the *Russians* believe he drowned. They know he didn't defect to *us*. We have checked this carefully. Yet, here he is in the middle of a project backed by the Cubans. Obviously, the Cubans are not telling the Soviets what they are up to."

The Chairman's voice interrupted. "Are you suggesting that the Cubans are developing a nuclear device? A weapon?"

The lights came on.

"In its way, Chairman, this would be the perfect weapon, a weapon that man has lusted for, dreamed about, warred over, and even prayed over for more than five thousand years. All in all, this is quite a tale. . . ."

II

Harry Desceau located the group lingering over a late lunch on the hotel patio.

"Are you people connected with Firebird?"

His presence seemed to startle them.

"Yes," said the black man. "Why?"

"I'm here to do something I hardly ever do."

"What's that?"

"Apologize." Desceau smiled broadly. "Forgive me. My name is Harry Desceau. I'm president of Cinabre. It was my people who gave you the hard time. I'm sorry about that."

"We worked it out," Magraw said dryly.

Desceau laughed. "I know you did. You made fools of them. You understand, I hope, that we've had more than our share of difficulties up there, and our people are a little edgy." He seemed nonplussed by the group's unresponsiveness. "Say, let me buy you folks a drink."

"Please join us," said Magraw.

"Thanks, I think I will." He hailed a waiter, ordered drinks, then pulled up a chair.

When Magraw introduced himself and the others, Desceau looked disappointed. "Oh, I thought Mr.—Wolfram, is it—would be here."

"He had to get back to Washington. Business," said Magraw.

"That's too bad. I wanted to meet him, perhaps do some business with him. He's the president, isn't he?"

"That's right."

"Well, another time, then." Desceau shifted in his seat. "Firebird . . . you do oil-well work, is that right?"

"Not exclusively."

"You know, I had to laugh at the way you turned the tables on my security people. Marines couldn't have done it better."

"Luck and desperation," said Juanita. "When we saw the courier with our briefcase, we assumed, of course, that he was a guerrilla."

Desceau's eyes narrowed. "That was a bit of good fortune for you, wasn't it? Coming along in the middle of the night that way, I mean. Unusual."

"The best time to travel," Juanita said smoothly. "The daytime heat is so oppressive."

Their drinks arrived. Before the waiter left, Desceau ordered another round. "What kind of work were you doing up on the Flan?"

"Seismographic studies," said Kinsey.

"Of what sort?"

"Primarily, we were measuring the P and S waves emanating from a specific charge of high-energy explosive—something like C4 or composition B."

"But what were you measuring up on the Flan?"

"Hard to say. We merely make the readings. Somebody else interprets them."

"I'd hate to think that Cinabre might be—threatened—by a competitor." He looked across his empty glass at Juanita. "You and your boss were getting close to Cinabre."

"We were? Just where *is* Cinabre?" Juanita asked.

"One more lake down the line from where you happened on the courier."

"I'd love to see it," she said. "I've never been inside a mine."

"Perhaps we can work something out." He turned to Harada and Kinsey. "What about you two? Would you like to go into the mine?"

"Not me," said Kinsey. "Flying's my business. I like lots of sky around me."

"Were you the fellow who flew over our lake a week or so ago?"

"Might have. I flew around the Sierra de Flan to line up landing sites."

"No trouble, I hope."

"None," Kinsey lied. "Why?"

"The Cinabre guards are nervous. Sometimes they shoot without thinking." Desceau looked around the table. "Counting the missing Mr. Wolfram, there are five of you. My people told me there were only four of you up on the Flan." He shook his head. "It seems they can't count, either."

Harada spoke up. "I wasn't there."

Desceau looked puzzled. "No?"

"I went sightseeing in Chichicastenango. Fascinating. Have you been there?"

"I'm not much for touring." Desceau stood suddenly. "I must be going now. It's been a pleasure meeting you. Again, I apologize for the misunderstanding."

Magraw held up his palm. "Forget it."

"When will Mr. Wolfram be back?"

"A couple of days."

[85]

"Will you people be doing more work up on the Flan?"

"Can't tell," said Magraw. "It depends on whether our client wants us to take more readings."

"If you do go back, let me give you a word of advice."

"What's that?"

"Stick to the high country. It would be a shame if one of my patrols hit you down below. They have this terrible habit of shooting first, then asking questions."

III

In Washington, the meeting droned on. Various members of the group enlightened their colleagues about several different companies owned and operated by Desceau, including a trucking enterprise traveling the Inter-American Highway between Guatemala City and Dallas, a small-scale smelting and precious-metals recycling firm in Dallas, and a Dallas-based commercial agent and broker who regularly bought and sold metal commodities.

"So, gentlemen," the tall man summed up, "you have the book on how Desceau and his Cuban friends will ship their 'mercury' into the United States. It all seems rather straightforward, doesn't it? But, of course, there is more. Thome?"

An exceptionally thin man to Wolfram's left stood and bowed slightly before making his way to the dais. Wolfram recognized him as Dr. Basil Thome, one of the country's leading authorities on nuclear reactors.

The physicist stumbled slightly as he reached the rostrum, recovered, and smiled apologetically before beginning. "My part in this came about when my staff was invited to make a routine metallurgical analysis of the steel tubes you see on the table here. When brought to us, one tube was empty. The other was capped and filled with what apparently was mercury.

[86]

"The mercury was put aside and the tubes were subjected to analysis by electron microprobe. It was determined that the metal was type 301 stainless steel, a conventional alloy."

Dr. Thome's high, reedy voice was not very pleasant to listen to, Wolfram decided. He wished the man would get to the point.

"Next, we submitted the mercury to the microprobe and we got a rather startling surprise. To explain it, I'll have to give you a bit of background in nuclear physics.

"As you'll recall from your college chemistry, the characteristics of any element are determined by the number of protons in its nucleus. Its mass, on the other hand, is determined by the number of protons plus the number of neutrons. The neutrons, therefore, add mass, but do nothing to alter the chemical characteristics of the element. Thus, an element with one proton is always hydrogen, with eight protons, is always oxygen, with eighty protons, is always mercury. This is true regardless of how many neutrons are in the nucleus.

"If the number of protons changes, the element becomes another element. This can happen naturally in the case of some elements, such as radium. It can be induced, also, by nuclear bombardment. We call both of these processes transmutation."

Thome cleared his throat before continuing. "Now, mercury, as I indicated, has eighty protons. However, it occurs naturally with varying numbers of neutrons in the nucleus. We call these variations isotopes. In nature, mercury occurs as a mixture of these isotopes, one of which is mercury 200, accounting for 23.1 percent of the total. When we subtract eighty *protons* from this mass number, we are left with one hundred and twenty, which is the number of neutrons in the isotope. Is that clear?"

There were murmurs of assent. Wolfram wondered how many were assimilating it at all. His own interest was growing.

"Very well," Thome continued, "when mercury 200 is inserted into a nuclear reactor, it enters into what we call a neutron flux—a veritable deluge of billions of free neutrons going every which way.

"In this environment, the mercury 200 isotope captures one of these neutrons and, by simple arithmetic, becomes a new isotope, mercury 201—still with eighty protons, remember, but now with a hundred and twenty-one neutrons.

"But it so happens that this mercury 201, when excited, as it is in a reactor, throws out a proton, leaving us with seventy-nine *protons* and a hundred and twenty-one neutrons.

"Since we have changed the number of protons, we have changed the nature of the element. These are no longer atoms of mercury, but atoms of the substance with seventy-nine protons in the nucleus."

Thome fumbled with the brown paper bag, managing to drop it on the floor in front of him. Out of it rolled a bright yellow lump.

"And that substance, gentlemen, is *gold!*"

Chapter Nine

I

The room buzzed with comments and exclamations as Dr. Thome bent down to pick up the gold lump and put it on the table.

"Question!" Wolfram said. "If it's so simple to make gold out of mercury, why is the price of gold going up? Or is that part of our national monetary strategy?"

"I know nothing of national strategy," Thome replied. "But I do know that we are not 'making' gold in our own reactors on anything but a small, experimental scale. This transmutation of mercury 200 to gold 200 is subject to certain realities of nuclear physics. I won't bore you with those in detail. In essence, in *our* reactors our experiments produce only minute quantities of gold 200 from mercury. This is true of other isotopes as well. You must remember that there are billions of atoms, only a small percentage of which are actually impacted by neutrons in our systems."

"In other words, you can't do what this Karuchkin can," said the Chairman.

"We haven't really tried," Thome protested. "We're not medieval alchemists."

"What would it take to do it?"

"At the very least, it would require a high-flux isotope reactor of the type we employ at Oak Ridge. It would have to be equipped with an extremely well designed neutron reflector, a kind of hall of mirrors to bounce the neutron flux back and forth repeatedly to multiply its effect. Obviously, in this case, such a design has been accomplished."

"I saw that tube opened," Wolfram interjected, "and what came out looked like pure mercury to me."

"What you saw," Thome responded, "was a mixture—an amalgam—of unaffected mercury atoms and gold atoms. We had to separate the gold chemically, a simple process. But to the naked eye the amalgam would look like mercury."

Of course, thought Wolfram, Desceau would ship the material into the United States as mercury and separate it here.

"We've got to have that design," said the Chairman. "Do you have the remotest idea of the impact this could have on the world economy? Do you have the faintest idea how many nations—including ours—count gold as part of their monetary reserves? And this group of Cubans and a renegade Russian are threatening the whole business."

Policy making was obviously not Dr. Thome's area of concern. He looked totally mystified by the Chairman's remarks, and asked to be excused from the rostrum. As he resumed his seat, the tall man who had been chairing the meeting rose.

"The Chairman has raised a rather essential question," he said, looking around the room. "And the answer is unequivocal: If this process continues outside our control, it represents a number of threats to our interests.

"In the first instance there is the matter of the Cubans piling up vast sums of world currencies for God knows what purposes, assuming they keep their scheme secret.

"But a greater threat is the potential damage the revelation of this thing could have on the stability of many economic systems and currencies, including our own, both directly and indirectly. After all, mercury costs only fifteen to eighteen cents an ounce, while gold is worth more than a hundred times as much presently."

"But," Thome cried, "all physicists know about transmutation. And they know about the gold-200 isotope. Lord, there are more than *twenty* isotopes of gold. We've made them all."

[90]

Something glittered in the Chairman's eyes. "And how many of them are stored in Fort Knox?"

"That's stupid."

"The trouble with you scientists is you can't gauge the difference between theory and practice, between what's meaningful to you and what's meaningful to human beings."

"We're not spies and killers."

"What about the atom bomb?" the Chairman replied, his voice filled with venom.

"Chairman, Chairman," the tall man pleaded. "Let's attack the problem, not each other."

After a moment of chilly silence, Thome continued. "There is another characteristic of gold 200 that would be a serious problem in mass production. It's intensely radioactive as it comes from the reactor."

Wolfram sat bolt upright. "My people and I *handled* that stuff!"

Thome turned to face him. "You're Wolfram, aren't you?"

"Yes."

"We considered your problem."

"Are we alive or dead?"

"No problem," Thome said. "But you're lucky."

"Why don't you explain it, Doctor," the tall man suggested. He pointed at the gold nugget on the table. "Is it dangerous?"

Thome stood up by his chair. "Our sample here—weighing just under one kilogram—is not at all dangerous. *Now.* But when it was fresh out of the reactor, each gram of this gold 200 contained nearly twenty million curies of gamma-radioactive material. And, as I've indicated, the tube contained about a thousand grams."

"Jesus!" Wolfram gasped. He looked at his hands.

Thome nodded. "Quite a lot, yes. In fact, enough at that moment to produce more than a hundred thousand roentgens of radiation per second per gram." He cleared his throat apologetically. "Of course, only a thousand roentgens of ex-

[91]

posure is absolutely fatal. Naturally, that is why, as Mr. Wolfram reported, the material was dumped into the lake. Water is a moderately effective shield against radiation, and the distance beneath the surface would provide an exponential benefit to those above." Thome looked directly at Wolfram. "But don't worry. You're safe. I think."

"You *think!*"

"Yes. You see, gold 200 has a radioactive half-life of only forty-eight point four minutes."

"Half-life?"

"One-half of the material's radioactivity dissipates in some forty-eight minutes, one-half of the remainder in the next forty-eight minutes, and so on. In the case of gold 200, at the end of one day, a kilogram of gold would be dangerous only if one were exposed to it for some time. At the end of two days, it would not be any more dangerous than an illuminated wristwatch."

"But I don't know how old the material we obtained was."

Thome nodded. "We have sensitive equipment. By measuring the residual radiation we worked backward and calculated that the material had been in the lake about three days when you recovered it."

Wolfram sighed in relief. But how close did Juanita get to the fresher material? The tubes they had seen dumped had been in the water only a matter of hours when she dived near them. The water—and distance—would have shielded her, of course—but enough?

The tall man took over again. "Well," he said cheerfully, "we have identified our problem. Now what do we do about it?"

The Chairman spoke up. "We've got to kill that golden goose. Immediately."

Wolfram disagreed. "Why not just sidetrack this mercury amalgam when it's imported, take the gold and substitute plain mercury?"

"It doesn't hit the source," said the Chairman. "We'd hit

them once and they'd find other channels in other countries. And it would tip them off that we knew they had the Midas touch. I'm afraid we're going to have to take more fundamental action."

The tall man addressed the Chairman. "There is only one problem. Congress has put a rather clammy *mortemain* on our active operations, you see. We . . ."

The Chairman interrupted. "You want the Bank to do your work because we're outside the government, right?"

The other man's expression was pained. "Exactly. Naturally, any material you might recover would accrue to the Bank's account."

"I won't quibble. I'm as anxious as you are to smother this thing. God! Gold at eighteen cents an ounce! We can't afford to have a bunch of outsiders holding the keys to the supply-and-demand equation for gold. It's my guess the Soviets don't want it, either. That's why Karuchkin and the Cubans cooked up this disappearing act."

"We have not entirely eliminated the possibility of Soviet involvement."

"Well, eliminate it now. They're no more interested in a way to make penny gold than the Arabs want to develop solar energy. They're probably the world's biggest gold producer. It's one of their major sources of foreign exchange. They need high-price gold."

"What do you suggest?"

The Chairman swiveled toward Wolfram. "You've been to Cinabre. Talk about it."

Wolfram moved to the rostrum. He described for the group the terrain problems, the difficulties of access to the Cinabre site, the earthquakes, the guards and their arms.

"If," he concluded, "you want to get the details of this reactor before you wreck it, you'll have to get inside the mountain. That would take an armed assault. At least a platoon of Rangers with mountain training."

"Out of the question," said the tall man. "Our 'clients' in

Guatemala don't have that level of proficiency, and we dare not use our own people."

Wolfram shrugged. "All right. The other alternative is simply to shut the thing down. It would mean getting well above the mine site on the mountain and starting a landslide with explosives. However, success might be transient. They might be able to dig back in. Of course, there is a good chance such a move would eliminate Karuchkin, assuming he would be there. He's the key to the whole operation. They couldn't repeat their arrangement without him if we wrecked it *and* got him."

"That's terrible!" Thome exploded. "He's a scientist. You can't just contrive to murder him."

"What do *you* suggest, Doctor?"

"It's none of my affair what you do. Start an earthquake, for all I care."

Wolfram stared at Thome. Suddenly, the physicist's facetious remark triggered something in Wolfram's mind. "About that earthquake, Thome . . ."

"What?"

"You'll have to join our expedition, of course."

"*Me?*"

"Definitely. Someone knowledgeable will have to read the reactor. And I'll need to talk to some seismologists."

"You can't be serious," Thome protested.

"But I am."

Chapter Ten

I

The Inter-American Highway took them through rolling, high mountain country studded with ranches, farms, and scattered pine groves. Forty miles from Guatemala City, Wolfram wheeled the truck onto another road, little more than a paved trail winding along the sides of canyons. Occasionally they passed colorfully dressed Quiché Indians beside their little thatched huts or tending corn patches.

Basil Thome had no interest in any of this. He was still trying desperately to adjust to the pace of events that had catapulted him out of his quiet nuclear energy research project and into a Central American hinterland. Of more specific concern to him were the wooden crates tied into the back of the truck, each bearing a stenciled label—SEISMOLOGICAL EQUIPMENT or TOOLS.

"For God's sake, Wolfram! Slow down!"

Wolfram glanced over at the scientist. "Relax. The stuff in back is perfectly safe."

"Please! Watch the road."

"There's the lake," said Wolfram as they rounded a curve.

Thome saw a vast stretch of water reflecting mottled tones of blue, green, and gray. "Volcanoes," he said grimly.

"The big one is Atitlán. The lake is named for it. Next to it is Toliman. The smaller one is Cerro de Oro."

Thome felt queasy. The sight of the volcanoes had done nothing to settle his already churning stomach.

"Can we stop? My insides are . . ."

Wolfram pointed ahead. "We're here. That's Panajachel."

They rolled slowly down the main street, then turned left on a dirt road that took them directly to the old coffee plantation. The helicopter was nestled in a large open area surrounded by small trees. The rest of Wolfram's crew were waiting beside the aircraft.

Wolfram drove the truck up to them and stopped. Thome wrenched open his door and stumbled out.

"Meet Dr. Thome," said Wolfram, getting out himself.

Magraw held out his hand to the scientist. "Welcome to Firebird."

"Thank you. I'd rather be somewhere else." Thome took a handkerchief from his pocket and mopped his mouth.

The Firebird group studied the odd figure dressed in a rumpled seersucker suit, a cotton shirt with its collar points curling up, and a thin knit tie dangling forlornly.

"Dr. Thome is going to assist us in the next phase of our project," said Wolfram.

"And what is the next phase?" asked Magraw. "Your message this morning merely said to be here."

Wolfram didn't answer him. To Kinsey he said, "Gassed up and ready?"

"When you are."

"You didn't answer my question," Magraw persisted.

"All in good time," said Wolfram. "But first we take the stuff from the truck and put it in the chopper. And then we take the chopper back to Alpha lake."

"Maybe we should get permission from Señor Desceau," said Juanita. "While you were gone he told us ever so nicely that we might get shot if we venture near Cinabre again."

"He *told* you?"

"Yes. He wants to meet you, Hugo. To talk business, he says."

She described the approach by the millionaire. "He has his eye on us. Someone probably is watching us right now."

Wolfram rubbed his chin. "I don't like it. What do you think he knows?"

"I think he knows nothing for certain," said Harada. "Our cover is as tight as truth. But that alone would trouble a type like Desceau."

Wolfram nodded. "Then he's going to keep after us."

"But what can he do without facts?" Kinsey asked.

"He doesn't need facts. I'll meet him. I'd rather be watching him face-to-face than looking for him in the shadows."

"I suggest you do it soon," said Harada. "Before he gets his traps set."

"Tonight. But first we get set up by Alpha lake. Then Kinsey can bring me back here."

"We still don't know what's going on," Magraw complained.

"I'll explain it when we get there. Now, let's get the stuff moved."

II

The Indian's Spanish was flavored with too much Quiché for Desceau to follow it easily.

"Slow down," he snapped. "Start at the beginning and tell me very carefully what you saw."

The Indian took a deep breath and began again. "This morning my friend and I went to watch the flying truck with the whirling top, as is my job."

"Go on."

"There were four people there, so we hid in the coffee bushes." The Indian described Juanita, Kinsey, Magraw, and Harada.

"Then what?"

"Soon came a large truck driven by a man with snow-white hair and many scars of the face. He was accompanied by another, a man like a skeleton with huge glass eyes."

The white-haired man was Wolfram. But who was the other? His information was that there were only five in the Firebird group. "What did they do?"

"They offered greetings to each other. Then many boxes were removed from the truck and put in the flying machine."

"What kind of boxes?"

"Wooden. About so big . . ."

"They could be arms," Colonel Guiteras said from the corner of the room. "They may be running guns to the guerrillas."

"Possible," Desceau replied. To the Indian he said, "After they put the boxes in the flying machine, what did they do?"

"They all flew away in the machine."

"I don't like this, Harry," said Guiteras.

Desceau stuffed a few bills into the Indian's hands. "Go back and watch that place. Come tell me as soon as you see anything." He waved the man out.

"We had better send another patrol up to the high lake," said Guiteras. "Perhaps I should lead it myself."

"And what are you going to do if you find them?"

"Take them prisoner, of course."

Desceau shook his head. "No, Colonel, I don't think that's a good idea." He stood and walked to the window. "The more I learn about this Firebird outfit, the less I know. That bothers me."

"I'm not squeamish," Guiteras said. "But this disposing of them—if that's what you are thinking of—could lead to inquiries."

"So we'll nip the inquiries in the bud. When you've got them all rounded up, you knock them out, put them in the chopper, and torch it." He turned to Guiteras with a smile. "Then Cinabre reports there has been a terrible crash and all were killed. Simple."

III

This time they made their base on the western side of the lake. No tents were set up. The wooden chests were stacked in the shelter of a copse of pines and covered with camouflage netting.

They unloaded the helicopter methodically and quickly. Basil Thome volunteered to lift and carry, but when he began to fumble a small chest of fuses, Wolfram sent him to the lakeside with a pair of binoculars and orders to scout for Cinabre patrols.

When everything was in order, Wolfram called the group together. Kinsey and Juanita broke out rations for everyone. As they ate, Wolfram told them what the cargo was.

"Two tons of C4 explosive," he said, "and the cleverest triggering devices you've ever seen."

"That's a lot of C4," said Magraw. "Why not something cheap, like dynamite?"

"And what is C4?" Thome asked.

Wolfram spooned down the last of his rations and put the can aside. "C4 is a plastic composition explosive, Doctor. It has several characteristics that make it appropriate for this exercise. First, it has excellent water resistance. Second, it is thirty-four percent more powerful than TNT. Third, it has an absolutely shattering detonation rate—twenty-six thousand feet per second. But before I get into the whys and wherefores of the C4, why don't you tell the others what's really happening with Cinabre."

Thome was startled. "What do you want me to tell them?"

Suddenly the ground shuddered beneath them, and Thome became even more edgy. "What was that?"

"That, Doctor, is the key to the mission," said Wolfram. "But, if you please. The isotope reactor . . ."

Somewhat diffidently, Thome described how the neutron flux in an isotope reactor bombarded common mercury into gold. When he was finished, there was silence.

"Questions?" asked Wolfram.

"What are we going to do?" Harada asked.

"The obvious problem is that we can't get at the reactor because it's inside a mountain and guarded by troops," Wolfram replied. "But if the reactor suddenly is ten or twenty feet under water, then the troops leave. Or they drown. At just that moment, Juanita and Dr. Thome swim into the cave, study the layout, make notes, take souvenirs, and leave."

"But I can't scuba dive," Thome protested. "I can barely swim."

"Doctor," Wolfram assured him, "that is why Juanita is going to spend the rest of today teaching you how."

"Okay for the swimmers," said Magraw. "How does the water get there?"

Wolfram stamped his foot on the ground. "What has been the one characteristic we've all noticed on the Sierra de Flan?"

"Earthquakes?"

"Right! And earthquakes will flood the Cinabre site—with a little help."

"I'm afraid, Hugo," said Magraw, "that you're going to have to explain this one *very* carefully."

"From the seismographic work we've been doing over in El Petén, we know that earth shocks produce two seismic waves. One is the P wave, which is not important to us. The other is the S wave, which is. . . ."

Wolfram picked up a machete and thrust it upright between two heavy stones.

"Now, the S wave works like this." He pressed the palm of his hand flat against the butt of the machete. "As I pull back the machete, friction between my palm and the handle makes the machete blade flex in the direction I pull. But I get it back only so far. . . ."

The butt slid from his palm and the machete flew forward, then back again, vibrating rapidly, ringing like a tuning fork.

"The same thing is happening all over Guatemala. Especially here on the Sierra de Flan. Huge formations of rock, along fault lines, are pressing against enormous friction in opposite directions. The tension builds and builds, then lets go suddenly, like the machete. There's an enormous release

[100]

of this energy that has slowly built up. That makes S waves—S for 'shear.' Earthquakes."

"Intriguing, Hugo," said Harada. "But how does that solve the problem?"

"Ahhh," said Wolfram, holding up a finger. "Exactly what I asked the seismologists. You see, my first idea was to trigger an earthquake by setting off charges."

"And . . . ?"

"It would have had the wrong effect. Instead of starting something big, it would have relieved stresses prematurely and aborted a bigger shock.

"But, they said, if one could trigger a blast *as* a quake occurred it would actually propagate the S wave and multiply the effect. Like shoving a pendulum already in motion."

"Sounds a little 'iffy' to me," Magraw said.

"They did some very convincing calculations for me," Wolfram replied. "Of course, the element of chance timing is there. We don't know when we'll get an earthquake of sufficient volume to do some good. But in these mountains the seismologists have recorded an average of a Richter Scale Two tremor every fifteen minutes, and there is a moderately severe shock—say, a Richter Three—once or twice a day."

"Let me get this straight," said Kinsey. "You plant your C4 someplace, a quake triggers it, a bigger quake occurs, and . . . what?"

"We don't just plant the C4 'someplace.' We plant it down there." He pointed toward the lake's outfall. "If the calculations are even close to being correct, the effect will knock the lip from the natural dam, maybe ten to twenty feet." He waved his arms. "Look! This lake has ten times the surface of little Gamma lake. So you drain ten feet from this one and feed it rapidly into the lakes down below and there is a rapid rise in the water level there. Temporary, to be sure, because some will flood right on out the other end. But there'll be enough to flood Cinabre and wash out the guards. Then we go in."

[101]

"I think it's insane," said Kinsey.

"At last, a sane voice," Thome added. "Frankly, I seriously question those calculations."

"But seismology isn't your field any more than it is Mr. Kinsey's, it is, Doctor?"

Thome said nothing.

"Very well, then. Kinsey and I are going back now for my rendezvous with Harry Desceau. We'll see you in the morning."

Chapter Eleven

I

Harry Desceau was fixing himself a drink in his living room when Guiteras burst in.

"Harry, there is news! Our people . . ."

Desceau turned to him, annoyed. "Calm down, Guiteras. Have a drink?"

"There is new information. About Wolfram."

"Oh?" Desceau strolled to the window. "Something happen to him?"

"We don't even know where he is."

Desceau seemed unconcerned. "What's the news?"

"There is a strong chance he is an American agent." Guiteras looked over his shoulder as if expecting an eavesdropper.

Desceau put his glass down. "What's the evidence?"

Guiteras sat down in one of the big leather-covered chairs and composed himself. "I must confess that I was dissatisfied with your appraisal of this Firebird organization as just a corporate competitor."

"So?"

"As a consequence, I took the investigation into a new channel. It took more time, but we do have a report."

"Let's hear it."

"Very well." Guiteras took the glass of Scotch Desceau offered him. "As you know, our intelligence organization has maintained a close liaison with"—he leaned across the bar confidentially—"the Soviet KGB."

Desceau's jaw muscles tightened. "So?"

"We asked our friends in the KGB to . . ."

"Are you out of your mind?" Desceau slammed his empty glass against the bar. "We been ducking the KGB for years! If they get one sniff that Karuchkin is still alive, the Red Army will be marching over the Sierra Madre!"

Guiteras held up a palm. "Please, please, Harry. We told the KGB nothing of any of this. They know nothing of Cinabre in Guatemala. We merely advised them that this Firebird organization was operating in Guatemala. In El Petén. And they were. We told the KGB we were concerned about them because of their work with explosives. We were very discreet, very plausible."

Desceau splashed more whiskey into his glass. "And what did the KGB find out?"

"They reported that they did have a file on Hugo Wolfram. Nothing specific, but they said that he and his group were often in very suspicious proximity to certain events that had turned out badly for Soviet interests. They believe that Wolfram is a well-covered American agent—perhaps his whole organization besides. They have never been able to place him in the American *aparat*, however. He may be an auxiliary of some kind."

"Meaning what?"

"Meaning his cover is very good, or he is what he purports to be—or both." Guiteras considered his glass thoughtfully. "We must add to these factors the matter of your own . . . involvement with the U.S. Government. You are a problem for them. Isn't it likely that they would send agents to Guatemala to shadow you?"

"What's to shadow? I'm an open book. Hardly a businessman in the country doesn't get indicted once in a while. But the U.S. Government isn't going to send the marines to Guatemala for Harry Desceau."

"But your problems would call attention to Cinabre, would they not?"

"Why? I have two dozen operations going, some of them right under their noses in the States."

"According to our experience, domestic legalities do not trouble them abroad," Guiteras suggested dryly.

Desceau conceded the point. "All the more reason to carry through with our plan. And all the more reason to make it look like an accident."

"I agree. But I believe we should detain one or two of them for interrogation, nevertheless. This Wolfram would be the ideal subject."

Desceau was about to reply when one of the gate guards entered.

"What do you want?"

"A message for you, sir."

The guard handed him a piece of hotel stationery. Desceau read the note quickly and shook his head.

"What is it?" asked Guiteras.

"Listen." Desceau read, " 'Will you join me for dinner to-night? Eight P.M. Black tie. Hugo Wolfram.' "

Desceau scribbled an affirmative reply on the bottom of the note and handed it back to the guard. "Take it to Señor Wolfram at the hotel. *Pronto!*"

Guiteras looked distressed. "What could he want?"

"What we both want," Desceau smiled. "Eye contact."

II

A black shape trudged out of the lake and up onto the shore. Juanita came over and removed the mouthpiece under the diving mask. "You did just fine, Dr. Thome. I believe you've got the idea."

Magraw helped Thome out of his tank harness.

"It's rather fun after one learns how to breathe," said Thome. "But quite cold."

Juanita patted him on the shoulder. "You're a good student, Doctor." She looked at his hands. "Where is your lantern?"

Thome, teeth chattering, muttered something unintelligible. "I'm terrible about these things," he told her. "Just terrible."

"You left it in the lake."

"Yes."

"Then you will have to get it."

Thome seemed confused. "And I thought I was doing so well."

"You're doing beautifully. Except for the lantern. Did you leave it on or off?"

"Off," said Thome. "I think that's why I forgot it."

From her own equipment, Juanita retrieved her lantern and gave it to him.

He looked balefully from her to Magraw and back. "This is all insane, you know."

Magraw grinned. "Who would think trying to turn mercury into gold was anything but the dream of a madman?"

Juanita stuck the scuba mouthpiece between Thome's teeth. "Down you go! And this time, bring back both lanterns."

As Thome returned to the lake and disappeared, Magraw sighed. "Can he make it?"

"He'll be all right. He's just awkward. But he doesn't panic. I'll be with him—and Wolfram, probably."

"Harada and I have been going over the written instructions on the triggering mechanism and the C4 inventory. There's enough of that stuff to knock the dam out without an earthquake."

"It'll probably take all of the C4," she said. "That dam was put there by an earthquake, and there are many, many tons of rock that have withstood a lot of earthquakes since."

"Still, I think I'll try to get Hugo to hold some back."

"Why?"

"I think it's risky to multiply natural forces this way. Sup-

[106]

pose we get more than we bargained for and the whole thing goes. Hell, we could flood everything between here and the Pacific."

III

Wolfram had ordered dinner in the same private room that he and the Firebird group had used, but this time the large table was set for only two. Candelabra cast a soft yellow light on the serving plates and silverware. In one corner a pair of waiters stood by a portable bar.

Precisely at eight a hotel official ushered Harry Desceau into the room. Like Wolfram, he wore a dinner jacket and black tie.

"You're a prompt man. I'm Hugo Wolfram." He extended a hand.

Desceau, unsmiling, took it. His grip was firm, his hands were large, larger than Wolfram's. The pale light from the candles reflected from his eyes but cast his face in shadows. They made him seem leaner than he was.

"If someone invites me for dinner at eight o'clock," he said, "I assume he means eight o'clock."

Desceau appraised Wolfram. This, he told himself, is a hard man. Candlelight didn't flatter the scarred face. As tall as I am, Desceau observed. Not so heavy. Wirier. And in better shape.

"Have a drink," said Wolfram.

"Scotch," Desceau told the waiter. "Ice, but no water."

Wolfram ordered the same.

Desceau looked around the room. "I thought some of your people might be here, too."

"They're up in the mountains. My pilot brought me back for this."

The waiter brought them their drinks.

"What mountains would they be?"

[107]

"Sierra de Flan."

"I'm glad they're not afraid to go back. Nice people you've got—met them the other day."

"They told me."

"That's how you knew I wanted to meet you."

"They said you wanted to talk business. I'm a businessman and I like to talk business. I happen to think the best time to talk business is over a couple of cigars after a good dinner."

Waiters wheeled in food-laden carts and arranged appetizers on the table.

"Looks good," said Desceau.

"Hungry?"

"Always." The larger man glanced at Wolfram. "You must be starved yourself. It's a long day flying down from the States, out to the Flan, and back."

"Not too bad. I had to go north and check with my client on this project."

They sat down and ate their appetizers, then the soup, in silence. The main course was a local beef ragout. The waiter poured a Chilean red wine for them.

After a time Desceau said, "It's none of my business, but who is your client?"

Wolfram sipped wine. "A big outfit. We're doing seismographic work for them."

"A big outfit without a name?"

"Sorry."

The waiters cleared the dishes of the main course, then put a flan dessert before them.

Desceau played with his spoon. "This is what they named our mountain for. In fact, the dessert is steadier than those damn ridges."

"How do you protect your mine against the shocks?"

"Cinabre?" Desceau spooned up his dessert. "We took advice from the Mayas. All the concrete members are built to have sliding surfaces at the angles instead of rigid joints. We use a lot of prestressed concrete that can take a severe shock.

[108]

When we get a quake, everything slides a little bit, but it doesn't break."

"And how is the mine doing?"

Desceau eyed him suspiciously.

"Don't worry," Wolfram chuckled. "My client isn't interested in mercury."

The waiter cleared the dessert dishes, then set out bowls of fruit and boxes of cigars. A cart of brandies was wheeled up. Each man selected a meduro claro.

"Shall we talk a little business, Mr. Wolfram?" Desceau cut the end from his cigar and used one of the candles to light it.

"At your service."

"I'll be very frank. The directors of Cinabre are upset about Firebird's presence so close to the company operation."

"We got that impression from your guards the other day."

"Well," Desceau said slowly, "they overreacted. We're sorry about that." Desceau drew heavily on his cigar and puffed a ring toward a candle. "You see, Guatemala's a tough place these days."

"I've heard." Wolfram lifted his brandy. "Now, what kind of business did you have in mind?"

"It occurred to me that an arrangement could be worked out for Firebird to do its work in some other part of the country."

Wolfram's eyes narrowed. "I don't think I understand."

"You're an intelligent man, and you have good people working with you. But if too many other companies start poking around up on the Flan, we're going to have all the guerrillas in Guatemala to contend with."

"But what about my clients?"

Desceau shrugged. "Tell them you found nothing of interest."

"Can't be done. All I do is make seismographic tapes. They interpret them. They have trained geologists and they'd spot a phony in a minute. The other side of it is, maybe there's nothing there, anyway. If that's the case, they won't be back."

Desceau put his cigar down and looked directly at Wolfram. "Hugo, I say this with great hesitation. . . . It would mean a great deal to Cinabre to have you move out. At the very least, it would mean a considerable savings to us in security costs."

"Are you suggesting you might buy us out of this contract?"

Desceau brightened. "Right! We'd like to buy out your contract. You could go to work for Cinabre. We have a few projects in Honduras. . . ."

"Sorry," Wolfram interrupted. "Can't be done. I appreciate the offer, but we have a long-term commitment with these people. They'd sue me into the ground. But I'll tell you this, we have only three or four more days of work up there. Then we'll be gone."

"Will your clients be back?"

"It's hard to say. Even if the seismographic readings were positive, it would still take them months to organize a test drilling operation. They have to get core samples to see whether it's commercially feasible to go to development. That part takes years. They might be after nickel or copper. Who knows?"

Desceau puffed thoughtfully at his cigar. "All right," he said finally, "we've played the hand, and it seems I've lost." He looked out at the lake for a moment. "Listen," he said. "I don't want this acquaintance to end so abruptly. Have you ever seen a mercury mine?"

"No. Never have."

"How would you like to fly up to Cinabre with me tomorrow and take the tour?"

Wolfram felt a prickly sensation at the back of his neck.

"Well . . . I don't know. I was planning to rejoin my group in the morning."

"No problem. Come with me to Cinabre in the morning. We have our own floatplane. You can look over the mine, and then we'll fly you on up to the high lake to join your people. It's hardly out of your way."

Wolfram was leery. On the other hand, it would give him a look inside the Cinabre operation.

"Well . . ."

"Come on," Desceau insisted. "What can you lose?"

Wolfram relented. "Why not? I'd like to see it. What time?"

"Ten A.M. My car will pick you up. The plane is moored in front of my home." He stood up and extended his hand. "Thanks for the dinner."

"My pleasure."

IV

Kinsey was reading when Wolfram returned to the hotel room.

"How did it go?"

"Charming fellow. First he tried a subtle threat, then a bribe, and then he got very friendly. He invited me to visit Cinabre tomorrow."

"You're not going."

"But I am."

Kinsey dropped his book. "You'll never come out of that mountain, Hugo. Desceau isn't going to show you the golden goose and let you come back to tell the tale."

"I think he has something else up his sleeve. If he just wanted to get rid of us, he wouldn't telegraph his punches. I think he wants to find out who we are and what we're up to."

"And then dispose of us."

"Probably. But as long as Desceau's with me, he's not out looking for you."

"He has others to look."

"We can handle them."

"And how are we supposed to get you out?" Kinsey wanted to know.

"Forget that for the moment. Tomorrow you go back up to Alpha lake as planned. But I have some changes in the program, so listen carefully."

Quickly he gave Kinsey the details.

When he was finished, Kinsey shook his head slowly. "Now I know."

"What?"

"You've gone over the edge."

"Just be there to catch me."

Chapter Twelve

I

The C4 was a whitish plastic packed in blocks of two and a half pounds, eight blocks to a haversack. They squeezed ten pounds of the stuff into a long loop and wrapped it in nylon tenting. Then they wrapped the tube, along with loops of fuse, over Harada's shoulder and across his naked torso.

"Don't scuff your feet on the rug today," said Magraw. "One spark of static and you'll be competing with that Atitlán volcano."

Harada smiled. "Hugo says this stuff can't go off without the right caps."

"Here they are," said Juanita, holding up a shabby Indian brimmed hat. "The detonators are tucked into the hatband."

"Remember to stay damp," Magraw told him. "Keep your sandals wet. Otherwise, this dry mountain air . . ."

Harada nodded. "Don't worry."

Kinsey brought the rest of Harada's Indian costume from the helicopter. "Are you taking the pistol?"

"I'm tempted," said Harada, tossing the serape over his shoulder. "But if I get stopped by a patrol and they search me, it would only make trouble."

"How will you explain the C4?"

Harada smiled. "Don't worry. I'll make something up."

"It had better be good," said Magraw. "Now, is everyone clear on the schedule?"

They all nodded soberly. Wolfram's alternate plan had an air of desperation about it that they didn't like at all.

Juanita embraced him. "Be careful, *muchacho*. We'd like to hear your side of the story after this mission is over."

As Kinsey started the engines of the helicopter again, Harada put his hat delicately on his head and turned to the group. "Believe me, I'd like to be there to tell it."

II

Wolfram went armed, as usual, with nothing but a clear conception of what he intended to do. Even so, that clarity was smudged by the knowledge that his own intentions might not prevail.

Desceau's limousine delivered him to a pier jutting out into Lago Atitlán from a bulkhead in front of Desceau's mansion. The floatplane was moored at the end of it. Desceau stood relaxed and waiting near the shore.

"Beautiful morning," said Wolfram.

"Always is here." Desceau, dressed in a pale blue bush jacket, eyed Wolfram's old U.S. Army field jacket, mountain cloth trousers, and climbing boots. "Looks like you're ready for the high country. Only it's hot as hell at Cinabre."

"I thought you were in the mountains."

"Cinabre is between the mountains, in a valley," Desceau explained. "We're less than five hundred feet above sea level at the water's edge, but the mountains go up three or four thousand feet all around. Up there it's cool, even cold. Down where we are, it's rain forest."

"Then there's jungle around the mine."

"Not much on our side of the lake. The ridge is too steep and the rock slides clean it out. On the other side, it's flatter and covered with jungle."

"Interesting. Do the guerrillas ever try to move up that way?"

Desceau finished the drink he held and handed the glass to a servant standing by. "We pay them off when we can."

Wolfram smiled. "I thought they were all untouchable Communists."

Desceau was not amused. "One way or another, everybody can be gotten to. Shall we?"

They strolled down the dock to the plane. The pilot was already in his seat, and one of the passenger seats was occupied by another man.

"This is Señor Chávez," said Desceau. "He's an engineer up at the mine."

"*Buenos días,* Señor Chávez." Wolfram recognized him as Colonel Guiteras. The Cuban nodded and smiled, saying nothing.

Desceau climbed into the copilot's seat. "I can fly this thing," he said, "but I'm not much good on landings, so we'd better hope the pilot lasts."

It was supposed to be a joke. Wolfram laughed. The pilot laughed.

The cough and roar of the engine cut off further conversation. Minutes later, the plane swung out on the lake, then, engine gunning, skimmed on a line directly toward the volcanoes, and up.

III

Juanita and Thome were already in their diving suits when Kinsey returned after delivering Harada. It had taken less than fifteen minutes.

Magraw had opened all the crates of explosive. Haversacks of the C4 had been moved down near the water. Detonators were spread out on a damp blanket in gaudy patterns of red, white, and blue.

Magraw pulled Wolfram's written instructions from his pocket and studied them. "I think we can get the thing hooked up right. But I sure wish we had Hugo here to do the wiring."

As Kinsey unpacked his own wet suit from a trunk and began to work on it, he glanced down toward the lake where Juanita seemed to be explaining something to Thome. "Our resident nuclear genius could sure use a little coordination."

"I'll keep an eye on him." Kinsey zipped his jacket closed and pulled the tight hood over his head. "I guess we're ready."

"Let's get started, then." Magraw called in the others. They walked over, their swimming fins dangling from their hands.

"Okay," Magraw said, "let's run through the instructions once more. The most important thing is to plant your C4 inside the moraine, in crevasses and so on. It must be in close contact with the rock. If there isn't a natural crevasse, chop one out, if you can, with your picks. Then plant at least ten pounds of explosive—four blocks—in each contiguous mass. The idea of putting the C4 in tight contact with the rock is to transmit the detonation shock through solid material. If your charge is set so it's just exploding water, that's no good. Confine it. Tamp it over with loose rock or gravel. . . ."

"But hydrostatic pressure should help," Thome interjected. "Detonation in water would not be useless at all!"

"I'm afraid, Doctor," Magraw said patiently, "that Wolfram's instructions are quite specific on that point. The reason is that the earthquake S waves propagate very rapidly—miles in seconds—but they do it only through solids. They do not transmit through liquids. We're looking for *shock* from our detonation, not pressure."

Thome, unchastened, looked away.

Magraw went on. "After you have the explosives in place, inject two of these"—he held up some of the colored detonators—"in each mass. Put them in alternately—two reds, two whites, two blues. Always one color in each mass."

"What do the colors signify?" Juanita asked.

"Red is an instant detonator. White explodes a hundredth of a second later. Blue a hundredth of a second after that.

[116]

That's supposed to vibrate the rock and multiply the after-shocks. At least that's what the seismologists told Wolfram."

Thome shook his head. "And all of you must remember that I have questioned those calculations. Frankly, I think we should try an entirely different approach to this problem. The only thing that can remove that moraine is hydrostatic pressure. Now, I suggest that we place the C4 . . ."

"Doctor!" Magraw said firmly. "Our policy is to do it Wolfram's way."

"It just strikes me that I, as a physicist, should have some influence on these decisions. This clearly is a technical physical problem and you are going about it the wrong way."

The others were silent. It was clear that he had no support.

"Very well, then," he said with more than a trace of annoyance, "we'll do it 'Doctor' Wolfram's way. But if it fails, don't say I didn't warn you."

"We won't," Magraw replied. "Any more questions? No? Okay, then, here we go. Each of you take one haversack—two if you can manage them—detonators, and ignition wire. When you use it up, come on back, we've got . . ."

The ground trembled underfoot.

". . . plenty."

IV

Harada found himself in a gloomy forest of elfin trees and moss, a world where the temperature was always cool, rain fell frequently, and the altitude allowed enough air to nourish the trees and filter out the killing sun rays, but no more.

Kinsey had brought him down quickly to ladder level, on the steep west slope above Beta lake. He had dropped down, and then the helicopter had whisked away, leaving him in eerie silence.

He could not hear even the call of a bird. A few hundred

yards below, under the thick canopy of the rain forest, monkeys chattered and birds screamed, but here there was only the highland quiet.

From his kit bag he pulled the old pocket watch, part of his cover. It was the kind of watch a highland Indian might have.

Eleven A.M.

Wolfram had said the trail was higher up on the slope, where the brush thinned out. The same trail was used by the Cinabre patrol, but it also offered access into the mine site itself.

It was time to move along. Dusk was many hours away, but the trail was unknown. Patrols might be out.

Harada tugged his serape around him. The bandolier of C4 was as awkward as a crutch. He pulled his heavy hat down on his head and wondered if Wolfram's plan could possibly work.

V

Cinabre hadn't changed in those few days since he had seen it through the twilight. Even the guards appeared to be lolling in the same positions at the same angles.

Wolfram climbed out on the pier, Desceau and Guiteras behind him.

"I thought there'd be more dirt scattered around. Where do you dump the stuff you dig out? In the lake?"

"You could say that, yes," Desceau replied.

A man in a white smock hurried from the mine entrance. Wolfram recognized him as Karuchkin. Desceau hailed him. "Dr. Timothy, meet Hugo Wolfram. Hugo, this is our director of research."

As they approached, Karuchkin's face registered shock. "You are from the Firebird group?"

"That's right." Wolfram extended a hand. "Pleased to meet you, Doctor."

"You did not tell me you were bringing anyone," the physicist protested to Desceau. "You should have told me."

"Relax. I didn't have a chance to get the word to you. Hugo and I arranged this visit last night."

The Russian frowned. "He will go inside?"

"Of course," Desceau said smoothly. "We want Mr. Wolfram to see how a real mercury mine operates."

Karuchkin's face reflected little relief. There was a moment of awkward silence, which Wolfram interrupted. "Well, Harry? Can I proceed?" He looked at his watch.

"Of course, Hugo," Desceau responded. "I know you're on a tight schedule. Follow me."

They walked along the narrow-gauge tram tracks into the entrance, with Guiteras behind them. The tunnel was constructed with heavy steel and concrete beams. Incandescent lamps in the arched ceiling provided a dim light. The walls of the tunnel housed piping, painted different colors. The colors, Wolfram knew, were codes indicating what each pipe transmitted.

Some two hundred feet inside the mountain the tunnel opened into an enormous high-domed cavern crisscrossed with a prestressed concrete superstructure arranged in interlocking triangles, like an enormous geodesic hemisphere. At its high point Wolfram estimated it would top a six-story building.

"It looks like an underground bridge," he said to Desceau.

"Took us two years to build. It's more like a shock absorber." He pointed ahead. "And there's the pièce de résistance."

A pool sunk in the floor of the chamber under the dome measured at least a hundred feet on a side. The water in it was bright, still, and clear, illuminated from below.

Wolfram feigned ignorance. "What does the water do in mining mercury?"

Desceau turned to him, his expression grim. "I guess we can quit the charade now, Hugo."

Two armed guards appeared, one on either side of Wolfram. "The problem is," Desceau went on, "we know that you're on some mission to find out what Cinabre's all about."

[119]

"That's absurd!" Wolfram protested. He knew his performance fooled no one.

"Cut it out!" Desceau snapped. "As I was saying, we know you've been retained by someone to investigate our business. Guiteras here thinks you're American intelligence . . ."

Karuchkin, standing to one side, gasped, "Oh, no!"

". . . and I think you are a competitor trying to get a slice of whatever pie we have here." He chuckled malevolently. "It doesn't really matter what or who you are. You meddled in our affairs, and now we intend to give you the whole tour, including the grand finale."

"I can't believe this!" Wolfram sputtered. "It's outrageous! When my people hear . . ."

Desceau laughed out loud. "They won't." To the guards he said, "Search him!"

They did, but found nothing.

To Guiteras, Desceau said, "When you get back from your patrol, Colonel, I want you to interrogate Mr. Wolfram here, and then . . ." The Cuban nodded and left.

Karuchkin was clearly upset by the course of events. "I must know," he said. "Is this man KGB? If they know of this, *any* of this, they will come for us."

"Don't worry, Doctor. I have everything under control." Desceau looked at his watch. "I'm going back to Atitlán now."

"Do you really want me to show him the reactor?" Karuchkin asked.

"Why not? He's come this far." He smiled at Wolfram. "I'll see you later. Or perhaps not." He turned and walked back down the tunnel and out of the mine.

"What is going on here?" Karuchkin muttered when he was gone. "What has gone wrong?"

"Don't you know, Doctor?" Wolfram asked.

"Of course I don't know. It is madness."

"*Ne bespocoisia. Eto nevazhno.*"

Karuchkin's jaw dropped. The words were Russian: "Don't worry. It doesn't matter."

[120]

Chapter Thirteen

I

The narrow trail ascended from the forest level through a thicket of purplish nettles the Indians called *chichicaste*. None too soon, thought Guiteras. The rain forest heat was depleting everyone's energy. At the upper level it would at least be cool, and the foliage would be sparse.

The colonel looked back on his patrol. Nine men struggled up the slope behind him, sweating and gasping under their heavy packs, rifles, and bandoliers.

"Rest!" he ordered. "You may smoke." Guiteras motioned to his sergeant. "Send scouts ahead."

Guiteras squatted and watched the two scouts move out. He took a cigarette and lit it. Already he was fatigued, and they were no more than half the distance, if that. He checked his watch. It was well into the afternoon.

"Can we get to the high lake before dark, Sergeant?"

The man was one of those who had made the earlier expedition to contact Firebird. "It will be difficult, Colonel. The trail is rather easy from here until we get just north of the middle lake. But then the slope becomes very steep and we must descend again, following the rapids until we get to the high lake wall. It is very slow going there, especially with field packs. Last time we were traveling with blanket rolls only. We could not climb the rocks to the high lake in darkness."

Guiteras muttered a curse. "If only that lazy Desceau had started two or three hours earlier . . ."

There was a shout from far up the trail.

"Damn them!" Guiteras exclaimed. "Will these fools never learn military procedure! We must have *silence* on the march, Sergeant!"

The sergeant slung his AKM across his shoulder and jogged ahead, disappearing around a curve in the trail.

Guiteras finished his cigarette and sighed. Snuffing it out, he stood up and readjusted his pack.

The sergeant reappeared through the thicket.

"The men have a prisoner."

"A prisoner? A Firebird person?"

"No, sir. An Indian."

Guiteras made a face and sighed again. "Oh, very well. Let's move up, then." He stalked off as the sergeant drove the rest of the patrol to their feet.

Soon the colonel passed a break in the trail where the thicket opened up into the clearer upland. He saw an Indian, hands clasped behind his neck. The two scouts stood well back, their weapons trained on the man.

"At ease!" he ordered.

The scouts relaxed, to the Indian's visible relief.

"How did you apprehend him?" Guiteras asked.

"He was sitting beside the trail."

"Just sitting?"

"*Sí.*"

"You speak Spanish?" Guiteras snapped at the Indian. The man nodded, keeping his head down.

"What are you doing here?"

The Indian mumbled something.

"Speak up!"

"I look for work. They tell me there is a place by the small lake where there is work. A place the name of Cinabre."

"Who tells you this?"

The Indian pointed toward the north. "The tall people beside the flying machine."

Guiteras's eyes narrowed. "Describe this flying machine."

"This machine is very tall with an orange bird painted on

[122]

the side of it. The people did not look like *ladinos*. One was very black."

The Indian continued to keep his face down. His strange hat was pulled around his ears ludicrously. Guiteras sensed something familiar about him. Had he seen him before, working for Desceau, perhaps? But then, they all looked more or less alike.

"Where do you come from?"

"Over the mountains."

"Atitlán?"

"I have been there. I worked in Panajachel."

That must be it, thought Guiteras. The man had the look of some he had seen there. "How did you get so far away?"

"I walked."

Guiteras laughed and shook his head. It was true, of course, that these mad Maya roamed the highlands constantly. Still, one must take no chances.

"Did you search him?" Guiteras asked one of the scouts.

"No, sir."

"Do so!"

One scout handed his automatic rifle to the other and ran his hands over the Indian gingerly. He looked inside the man's shoulder bag.

"Nothing, sir. Only a watch and some Indian things."

"So you want to go to Cinabre, eh?"

"*Sí.*"

"Very well, one of my men will take you."

"I thank you."

Guiteras motioned one of the scouts over. "Take this carrion back down the trail," he whispered. "When you get into the jungle, shoot him. One shot. In the head. Understood?"

"*Claro.*"

"Get going!"

The scout went to the Indian and prodded him ahead with his AKM. "Follow the trail, *amigo*, I am right behind you."

"We are going to Cinabre?"

"Of course."

Guiteras watched the two figures walk past the rest of the patrol and disappear around a clump of *chichicaste*.

II

Wolfram was hustled quickly past the reactor and down a long neighboring corridor, where he was locked inside the Cinabre tool-and-parts cage. Karuchkin departed without a word, leaving behind a morose guard, who now watched him from the other side of the heavy-gauge wire mesh.

He checked his watch. There were still several hours before the tram, loaded with its cargo of radioactive gold, would roll out into the twilight. Once that hazard was safely dumped into the lake . . . Well, it would be close.

He looked around. The tool cage, about twenty feet by fifteen feet, was typical of any industrial operation. One side was the rock of the cavern; the other three were constructed of a heavy wire mesh fastened to steel uprights. The design, of course, facilitated close watch over the Cinabre inventory of tools. The array of tools was complete, mostly drills and automatic hammers ranging from very small to very large, along with the usual spectrum of wrenches, screwdrivers, chisels, and some cable.

It occurred to Wolfram that he had around him a vast assortment of potential escape devices or weapons. What he didn't have was a plan. A wrench would be no match for the guard's AKM, he thought.

Match! The word jarred something in his memory. A match. Matches!

From his pocket he took out the small waterproof canister of wooden matches that he always carried, a habit from commando days. He unscrewed the lid. The matches inside were the traditional strike-anywhere type.

He looked up at the top of the cage. The wall of mesh ex-

[124]

tended up about eight feet, just high enough to keep out—or keep in—minor troubles, but not high enough to withstand a full assault. The rock ceiling, buttressed by concrete beams, was too or three feet above the edge.

Wolfram glanced at the guard, leaning against the far wall of the corridor. The man's thoughts obviously were elsewhere, though he did glance at Wolfram from time to time. He noticed Wolfram looking at his matches.

"Do you have a cigarette, *amigo*?" Wolfram asked him.

The guard shook his head.

Okay, thought Wolfram, I don't smoke them, anyway, but at least you know why I took my matches out. Indeed, the matches had given him part of his plan.

Now it would be necessary to figure a way past the cage when the time came.

Wire cutter?

Slowly, he scanned the cage without moving from his spot. There was a bolt cutter, more than adequate for the job, but bulky. Even this daydreaming guard wouldn't stand by while he snipped the mesh. He rejected that idea for the moment.

The door to the cage itself might hold an answer. A Dutch door, it was solid on the bottom, with a narrow counter at waist level. The upper half was mesh. Both halves were padlocked on the outside, but the hinges were connected on the inside.

Wolfram ambled to the door and rattled it.

"Stop that," the guard growled.

"Sorry."

There were two hasps on the lower door held by pins at the hinge. The solid panel could conceal his hands while he pried the hasps loose from the wood. But it would be noisy, obvious work, and he couldn't unscrew the hasps without bending down.

What about the pins in the hinges? This was more like it. All he would need would be a quick pull with some long-handled pliers, if there were any.

That part of it was settled, then. Now to fashion the caps.

[125]

He wandered slowly, hands in pockets, and pretended to examine the oily bins of nuts and bolts. He picked up some at random and looked at them closely, as if interested in their dimensions.

"This is a big bolt," he said loudly to the guard, holding up one an inch in diameter. The guard shrugged and looked away. At that instant, Wolfram scooped up a handful of smaller bolts with nuts attached. Then he moved calmly back to the small desk and chair that served the toolroom clerk at other times, and sat down.

"No chair for you, eh, *amigo*?" he said to the guard.

"Quiet!"

"I am only concerned that you will get terribly fatigued standing there so long." He laughed. "I'm afraid you might decide to shoot me to save your legs."

"You are too noisy."

"Why not sit down, like me? Rest your legs. I won't tell them."

"Maybe you're right." The guard squinted down the corridor to see if anyone was watching.

"Of course I'm right," Wolfram encouraged. "Relax. I'm stuck here until Guiteras gets back, and that won't be until tomorrow."

The guard slouched down against the wall, cradling his rifle so that it pointed toward Wolfram. "No funny business."

"*Claro!*"

The little desk cut the line of vision between the seated guard and Wolfram's hands. He looked around to see if anything else suggested itself. A metal stepladder leaned against the wall. He stood and strolled over to it. He hefted it.

"Put it down!" said the guard. "Sit down."

"Sure." He turned rapidly, fumbled with the ladder, and dropped it to the floor with a crash.

The rifle muzzle swung his way.

"My apology. I'm a clumsy fool."

Wolfram leaned down to pick up the ladder, partially out

[126]

of sight of the guard. Quickly, he bent and broke off a piece of the soft, light metal. As he'd expected, it was magnesium. Most of these ladders were made of it.

He put the ladder back in place. Returning to the desk, he pushed and pretended to trip over an open wooden toolbox.

"What's the matter with you?" the guard demanded.

Wolfram pretended to struggle up to his feet. As he did, he thrust a file from the box up his sleeve. "This place is cluttered," he said, smiling apologetically.

Back at the desk, Wolfram found a piece of scrap paper and began the laborious process of filing the chunk of magnesium. After an hour, he had converted the soft metal into a small mound of whitish powder.

He was ready.

He glanced at the guard. The man's eyes were drooping. He wasn't asleep, but he wasn't very alert, either.

Wolfram removed the match container from his pocket and took out the blue-tipped matches. Next, he took the nuts and bolts from his pocket and put them on the desk.

Now for the delicate part.

Meticulously, he unscrewed one bolt until its nut was half off the end threads, leaving a cavity. Then, with his thumbnail, he clipped away the white tips from the blue bulbs of the matches. This material, he knew, was about one-third potassium chlorate, an igniter. He put several of the match tips into the nut cavity and topped them with a pinch of magnesium powder.

The cavity in the nut was partially filled now. He screwed another bolt into the threads so that he had two bolts fastened together by one nut, end-to-end. Very slowly, he tightened the bolts as hard as he could.

That done, he set about manufacturing another of these odd devices, and another, until he had made a half dozen. Carefully, he tucked these assemblies into his shirt pocket and buttoned the flap.

The hinge problem was next.

[127]

Wolfram stretched and yawned noisily. By stretching out his foot, he could reach the toolbox from which he had taken the file. Cautiously, he lifted his leg, hooking his heel into a corner of the box, and dragged it toward him behind the shield of the desk. At the same time he watched the eyes of the guard, who looked at him from time to time.

Inch by inch, Wolfram hauled the toolbox behind the desk where he could see its contents. There were several pairs of pliers. He selected a pair with a wirecutter and grooved jaws. His hand darted out, grabbed the pliers, and dropped them into his trousers pocket.

The sharp movement caught the guard's attention.

"Hey! What are you doing?"

Wolfram stood up slowly. "Just trying to keep from falling asleep, *amigo*." He moved toward the gate.

"Stay back."

"You are too tense, my friend," Wolfram said smoothly. "You must learn to relax in this life or you will quickly go into another."

"Away from the wire! *Pronto!*" The guard stood up, his AKM at the ready.

Wolfram backed up hurriedly. There was no doubt in his mind that the guard would fire. They faced each other for a moment.

At the sound of approaching footsteps echoing in the corridor, the guard came to attention. It was Karuchkin.

"Good afternoon, sir," the guard said diffidently.

Wolfram said the same thing, but in Russian.

Karuchkin held an automatic pistol.

Chapter Fourteen

I

The two of them, Harada in front, picked their way down the rocky trail. The actor knew he would have to make a move soon. Whatever Guiteras had whispered into the scout's ear, it portended nothing good for him.

The foliage was changing now from thickets to low jungle evergreens, and the temperature and humidity rose with every jarring step downward.

Harada stopped suddenly and held up his hand.

"What is it?" the scout demanded.

Harada turned to face the Cuban. He was a young man, perhaps twenty, of slight build. His jungle dress and equipment seemed too large for him.

"There is a custom among my people," Harada said piously.

The rifle muzzle swung upward and pointed to the actor's midriff. "Explain." The man's finger was on the trigger. The safety was off.

"Before we enter into the rain forest we must offer prayers."

"It's foolishness."

"Oh, please, sir. It is most important."

The scout was uncertain.

Harada beseeched him. "The jungle is full of ghosts and devils, as well as jaguars and reptiles. The prayers will protect us."

The Cuban laughed nervously. "You're a silly man. Our

patrol came by here less than an hour ago. We saw nothing."

"Indeed? But there were ten of you, all armed."

The Cuban shrugged. "Very well. Say your prayer, then. But be quick about it."

Harada squatted on his haunches and began singing a song. Actually, it was an old Japanese song, but as far as the scout was concerned, it was merely another obscure Mayan dialect.

From his pocket Harada withdrew some coins. Still singing, he began to do sleight-of-hand manipulations. He was careful not to look directly at the guard, but he watched him from the corner of his eye.

The youth's annoyance changed rapidly to amusement as Harada made his coins disappear and reappear.

"How do you do that?"

"Please don't interrupt. I am praying." In a real sense, Harada thought, it was true.

He resumed his singing, and continued his coin tricks, making the coins seem to disappear from one hand, only to reappear in the other. The full attention of the Cuban was focused on the graceful hands. The youth was leaning closer and closer to watch.

Harada changed his tune to a high, monotonous chant. Now a bright gold coin twinkled across his knuckles, flipping from finger to finger in flashes of reflected sun.

The young Cuban stooped to see, squinting now to slow the quick motion of the hands.

Slowly Harada made a quarter turn toward the entranced youth, singing and moving his hands as he did.

The Cuban was on his heels now, utterly fascinated. Now!

The coins flew into the young man's eyes. Instinctively, he ducked and blinked. The swift magic hands darted out, grasped his equipment harness, and yanked him abruptly, throwing him headfirst down the slope. His AKM clattered to one side as he sprawled on his back. Frantically, he twisted over on his stomach and scrambled to retrieve his rifle. But in an instant Harada was on the slim youth's back. His left arm girdled the Cuban's throat.

As for the rest of it, the actor's movements were automatic. Harada mentally counted the cadence of his motions in his mind: *Left* arm *in* place; *thrust* right *elbow* forward *over* opponent's *right* shoulder; *grasp* inside *right* elbow with *left* hand; *angle* back *forearm;* cup *base* of *opponent's* skull in *right* hand; *apply* pressure.

Harada squeezed his left forearm back and pressed his right hand forward. As his grip tightened, the youth's face turned beet red. His fingernails clawed at Harada's arm. Then he began to flail his arms and feet futilely against the hard earth of the trail.

One must watch the feet, Harada's training told him. The feet will fight for life until, finally, they signal death. The squeeze tightened still more. At last, there was a final jerk, and the youth went limp.

With one swift motion, Harada thrust the body aside, stood up, and retrieved the AKM. The corpse rolled a few feet down the slope, then flapped to a stop, face up against a copse of brush. In a final human indignity its bladder let loose, staining the military dress and the earth. A final comment, thought Harada, on what it all means. The bulging dead eyes stared an accusation at him.

This time Harada mumbled a real prayer in Japanese, bowing three times. After that, he dragged the corpse well into the thicket out of sight. With a switch of weeds, he brushed away all traces of the struggle.

II

Karuchkin motioned to the guard. "I intend to interrogate the prisoner."

"Colonel Guiteras will do the questioning when he returns," the guard sulked. He didn't like dealing with civilians.

"Go stand at the end of the corridor. I will call you when I am through."

"My orders are to stay with the prisoner."

"Damn you! Do as you're told!"

"Very well," the guard relented. "I will allow you five minutes."

"Colonel Guiteras will hear of this insolence, I assure you."

During this exchange, Wolfram edged up to the cage door. He reached down with the pliers and found a purchase on the flange at the top of the hinge pinion.

Good.

The guard strutted arrogantly down the corridor. Karuchkin snarled insults at the man's back.

Wolfram used the distraction to extract the pinion. He eased the pliers upward and dropped the metal rod into his other hand, then pocketed it.

The guard took a position some fifty feet away, then turned to watch both of them.

Karuchkin turned to Wolfram, pistol at the ready.

"I see you still carry a Soviet Tokarev automatic, Doctor," Wolfram said in English.

Karuchkin looked at the pistol and then at Wolfram. "You spoke to me in Russian before. Why?"

"Well, you were the one who seemed to be so upset about the KGB. I thought I was being friendly and reassuring."

"What makes you think I am Russian? Did Desceau tell you?"

"No, Desceau didn't tell me. But, as a matter of fact, it really is only the Russian who frets so about the KGB, isn't that so, Doctor?"

The scientist's hand was trembling slightly. "May people worry about such things. Why should you address me in Russian?"

"How did you know it was Russian?"

"I . . . No. *You* answer the questions."

"Turn the muzzle of that pistol elsewhere, then."

Karuchkin hesitated, then let his pistol hand fall to his side. "I warn you, I will shoot if you give cause."

Wolfram looked into the other man's eyes. "I could make up some plausible story, I suppose, but what's the point? You see, the fact is, we know who you are."

"We? Who is we?"

"*Not* the KGB."

"American intelligence?"

"Does it matter? Your secret is abroad in the world, and inevitably it will trickle back to the KGB. It's a problem for you, Dr. Karuchkin."

The scientist started at hearing his own name. "Karuchkin is dead. Drowned."

Wolfram laughed. "Whatever you say, Doctor. But when the KGB comes looking, who will you be?"

The physicist licked his lips. "Why do you insist on calling me Karuchkin? What makes you think I am he?"

"It doesn't matter. It's what others think at this stage of the game, isn't that so?"

The Russian brought the gun up to waist level again. "I want to know. *Now.*"

Wolfram pretended to shift his weight. He slouched against the narrow counter of the cage door. But the hand holding the pliers groped. He couldn't reach the lower pinion. He stood up straight again.

"Well?" Karuchkin demanded.

"Doctor," Wolfram said quietly, "why don't you consider . . . defecting from . . ." He gestured at the cave around them. "Siberia couldn't be much less pleasant than this."

Karuchkin's eyes narrowed. "It was fine enough until you and your people came. What I want to know is why? Why did you come? What could you know?"

"I suppose one could say that we came because we *didn't* know. We wanted to find out. And we have." He pointed a finger at the physicist. "I'll tell you something else, Dr. Ka-

[133]

ruchkin. I've read your file. You have a 'widow' and two children in the Soviet Union."

"Why did you come?" Karuchkin persisted.

"We were curious when we learned that a character like Desceau had teamed up with Cuban Communists. Don't you think that's an odd arrangement?"

Karuchkin said nothing.

"So we came to see," Wolfram continued. "And we find a Russian scientist who even the Soviet government thinks is dead. They would be *very* interested to learn that he is still alive, still working."

Karuchkin's face twitched. "The Americans would never tell the Soviets."

"You're wrong. Certain information is often traded when it serves our purposes. We give them a Chinese tidbit, they give us a Cuban tidbit. We give them information on Karuchkin, they give us . . . well, who knows? It depends how valuable they think you are. Then, of course, there is your family . . ."

"You'll be dead."

"But my people know, too. And many others. It's only a matter of time, Karuchkin. Like a paper bag full of water."

Karuchkin's breathing was labored. "I would never have left them if they had only accepted my ideas." His eyes pleaded with his prisoner. "I was rebuffed, reprimanded."

"*Our* organization will accept your ideas, Doctor. Why don't you come north?"

"Just who are you and your organization?"

The guard started to walk back. Wolfram touched his fingers to his lips. "There could be a way out for you, Doctor. The KGB need not know. Your family would be perfectly safe."

"I don't understand."

"At dusk," Wolfram said quickly, "after you have dumped the day's mercury into the lake, be beside the reactor. Under the dome."

[134]

"Why? I don't . . ."

"Just *be* there."

"Speak Spanish," said the guard. "This interrogation has gone on long enough."

Karuchkin turned on him savagely. "How dare you?"

The guard argued.

Good, thought Wolfram. Another momentary distraction. Quickly, he stooped and applied the pliers to the remaining pinion.

"Come up where we can see you!" the guard shouted.

Wolfram tugged.

"What are you doing there?"

The pinion came free, and Wolfram stood erect again, smiling. "My shoelace came loose." He slipped the pliers into his pocket.

The guard came close to the wire and peered inside. "Stay in view."

"Sorry," said Wolfram.

Karuchkin stared hard at him.

"Under the dome," Wolfram told him in English.

The scientist's face was pale. He put the automatic in his pocket.

"Good-bye," he said, turning.

"Da svedania."

III

The canyon above the middle lake was already in deep shadow as the patrol stumbled across the rocks and back-waters of the rapids below the high dam.

"We will need lanterns soon, Colonel," said the sergeant.

"No lights. Not yet."

"Do you intend to climb the bluff?"

"Of course." Guiteras looked at his watch. "Where is that fool scout?" He should have caught up with us hours ago."

"Perhaps he misunderstood the orders, sir, and went on back to Cinabre."

"Stupid," Guiteras muttered. "We should not have taken that long break to await him."

"Perhaps there was trouble."

"From the Indian? Nonsense." He gestured toward the trail ahead. "Let's move on, quickly. If we must, we will use the lights, but keep the noise down."

Guiteras, breathing hard and bone-weary, set the pace. The deepening gloom covered rocks and water. He was wet up to his waist and his knees were sore from slipping against the knobs of stone. Behind him he could hear the splashing and cursing of his troops.

Guiteras looked up. The sky above was still a bright blue ceiling for their tunnel between the mountains. Soon there would be full darkness here below.

It took them twenty more minutes to struggle up to the jumbled boulders at the base of the high lake's natural dam. It loomed above them, one smooth, black mass, illuminated sporadically by light reflected from the falling water. Here below, there was no place to bivouac. It was climb or turn back to some open space. When the patrol caught up and gathered around, he said, "All right, Sergeant. Break out your lanterns. We're going up. We will bivouac at the top."

The challenge in his voice dissolved as the ground trembled suddenly.

The sergeant laughed nervously. "If only this flan could be eaten, eh, Colonel?"

Guiteras, looking up, didn't answer.

IV

"Lights!" Kinsey whispered to Magraw.
"A patrol?"

"It's not a Boy Scout troop." The pilot hunched down behind a rim of rock at the top of the moraine. He hoped they hadn't seen his silhouette against the skyline.

They had completed planting the C4 several hours earlier. Juanita and Thome had been sent back to the helicopter to warm themselves and rest for the next step, while Magraw and Kinsey had remained to weave together the intricate ignition network for the explosives. The final step of that process had brought them to the jagged lip of the dam.

Magraw crawled up. "How many?"

"I count nine lights."

"They don't want to screw it up this time. Damn," he grumbled, "I thought everything was going too smoothly."

"What do we do?"

Magraw looked around. The daylight at their level was still fairly bright. "I've still got to hammer in those metal rods for the seismic actuators. This light isn't going to last much longer."

"Sure, but the hammering might shake them up if they hear it. They'll know we're up here."

Magraw nodded. "We'll have to muffle it. I can put cloth on top of the metal pickets, but there'll still be a thud. Maybe if you toss a stone over the side every once in a while, they'll think . . ."

They stared at each other. The same idea had occurred to both.

"Rocks!" said Kinsey. "The perfect weapon. We're loaded with ammunition."

Magraw clapped him on the shoulder. "Get to it, man."

It would be a long night of rock throwing, Kinsey knew. But no one in his right mind would climb up in the face of rolling stones. He hefted a ten-pound round stone and heaved it out and over his parapet. Fractions of a second later, he heard its first impact. Keeping his head low, he peered around his cover. He could see nothing in the darkness, but he heard another impact, a loud crack, then another, and another. There were other cracks as stones dislodged by the first tumbled somewhere into the darkness.

The bobbing lights seemed to freeze momentarily, then they scattered. There was a far-off cry. A hit?

From behind him came the heavy thud of Magraw's hammer against the long metal rod, one of the nerve ends of Wolfram's unique earthquake machine.

Kinsey tried a larger stone. It thundered into the depths, taking companions as it fell. Kinsey looked again. The lights seemed to be retreating down the gorge.

Now came the time of waiting.

PART THREE

" . . . and after the wind an earthquake . . . "

Chapter Fifteen

I

The warning horns blared, echoing down the corridor from the reactor chamber.

"What the hell is that?" Wolfram shouted at the guard.

The man straightened up but ignored him. At the end of the tunnel, lumpy, silver figures in protective hoods and smocks pushed shut a heavy steel door. There was the rasp of a bar on the other side. The closing clang muffled the sound of the horn.

Wolfram stood up from his chair by the little desk and thrust his hands into his pockets. The fingers of his right hand closed on two of the heavy bolt devices he had fabricated earlier. Casually, he moved away from the desk.

"What's going on?" he asked again.

"Not for you to know."

"Why was the door closed?" he demanded.

"Shut up."

If I bother him enough, thought Wolfram, the man will turn his back on me. "Why won't you answer me?"

No answer.

Wolfram calculated his movements carefully. There would be incredibly little time. He edged toward the door of the cage. Slowly, he withdrew his right hand from his pocket with the bolts clutched in his palm. He yawned noisily and pretended to stretch. His arms reached far above his head.

"Hey!" he called. "Is that door shut tight? It looks ajar to me."

The guard gave him a bored look, but turned to see for himself.

Now!

Wolfram flipped the bolts from his extended hand through the opening between the ceiling and the tool cage mesh. Following through on the same motion, he lunged forward on his hands and feet and scrambled for the cage door.

"Wha . . . ?" shouted the guard, catching the motion from the corner of his eye.

At that instant there were two almost simultaneous sharp cracks and brilliant flashes of green light. One bolt clipped the wire of the cage like a bullet and ricocheted against metal cabinets.

Wolfram clawed aside the lower half of the cage door and hurled himself through in a somersault that brought him up on his feet in a low crouch directly in front of the guard.

The Cuban, half blinded by the magnesium flashes, responded awkwardly. His hands fumbled at his rifle as he attempted to spin and cover his attacker. But he was too slow.

Wolfram brought his left knee up hard into the man's groin. His left hand grasped the man's hair and yanked his head down sharply. The edge of Wolfram's right hand hacked once, twice, at the exposed nape behind the ear, and the man plunged forward on his face, his rifle clattering against the cement floor.

It was all over in less than two seconds.

Wolfram staggered backward against the corridor wall and gasped for breath, his heart pounding.

He looked up at the ceiling and concentrated on bringing his body back under control. He sucked in drafts of air, then forced his breath out rapidly, only to gulp in another draft. Clear your mind, he ordered himself. He visualized a blank white door. Eyes closed, he stared at the door until he felt his thumping pulse begin in subside. He counted.

Soon it was close to normal. Then he looked down.

[142]

Blood oozed from the guard's ear. Wolfram stooped and felt the temple for a pulse. There was none. He examined his own right hand, opening and closing the fingers. It was all too easy for one to break a hand this way. The hand ached, but there was no serious damage. It would swell soon.

More deep breathing. He was under control now.

He rolled the body over and checked the AKM. Still on safety. The man carried extra magazines in pouches. Wolfram took one and tucked it inside his belt. Attached to the man's harness was a webbing holster containing a heavy flashlight. Wolfram took that, too, and buttoned it inside his shirt.

Then, holding the rifle at the ready, he walked slowly toward the closed metal door, staying close to the corridor wall.

The muffled honking continued. It seemed as if it had been blaring for hours. Actually, it had been only minutes. Wolfram held well back from the door, trying to sense what might be occurring on the other side. It made no sense to get close, for even the steel was scant protection from the massive amounts of radiation emanating from the fresh gold 200.

He knew that the tram somehow had to be hauled on its tracks out of the huge pool, then led down the main corridor to the lake. The warning horns would continue their racket until the discharge was completed.

Wolfram switched off the AKM's safety and put the fire selector on full automatic.

Now it was up to Harada.

II

The blue of twilight deepened. The Cinabre people would not be able to see him moving around in the brush now.

Harada moved slowly out of his concealment in the evergreens by the lakeshore. His trek down the mountain to this hiding place had been long and slow. The mine's engine house was still a hundred yards ahead of him, but the shoreline here opened up. It was, if anything, too open.

Quickly, he stripped off his Indian tunic and uncoiled the rope of C4 and fuse. He peeled away the plastic wrapping, pounded the whitish material into a lump the size of a small soccer ball, and punched his knuckles deep into the ball. The crudely shaped charge would focus the force of the blast in the direction of the cavity.

Now, at the mine mouth, silvery figures appeared, lumbering like robots, just as Wolfram had described them. They trailed cables behind. Somewhere back down the tunnel, Harada knew, the intensely radioactive cargo was in its tram, rolling toward the lake.

In this case Wolfram's instructions were very specific. Harada had to find a protective wall of rock or earth between himself and the tram, even if he already had the advantage of distance.

The actor found a hummock of fern-covered rocks that would protect him. Carrying the explosives and his other gear, he hunched down behind it.

The darkness was making his explosives chore more difficult. He removed the detonators from his hat and pushed them carefully into the side of the ball opposite the cavity. Then he attached a fuse to each detonator and a fuse igniter to each of them. The fuse was supposed to be waterproof, but the jungle dampness and perspiration had a way of finding chinks in the waterproofing. He hoped fervently this had not happened, for there wouldn't be time for encores. He would have to count on his multiple ignition trains to get at least one small spark to a detonator.

The honking continued. It would not be long now, he knew. His hand brushed the AKM. The weapon was a comfort, but did he dare carry it along? The thing was heavy, and it would be awkward running with a slung rifle bumping his backside. Reluctantly, he put it aside.

[144]

As he did, the horns stopped.

The ensuing silence seemed especially heavy. For an instant he hesitated, then looked over his shield of rock. The garbed figures were hauling the tram back from the pier. The spotlights could go on at any instant.

Harada, the ball of explosives hugged to his stomach, began to trot toward the engine house. With the sound of the horns gone, he could hear the steady thrum of the diesel once again.

As he jogged toward his target, he tried to keep the small building between him and the figures pulling the tram from the pier. The rocky terrain was not conducive to even moderately swift movement. Sharp edges poked his toes and rapped his shins.

Fifty yards covered. Seventy-five. The figures could see him now if they looked. It couldn't be helped.

Harada heard a muffled shout from one of the silver figures.

He'd been seen!

Still, they were much farther from the engine house than he, and hobbled by their protective suits. And they were unarmed.

Farther down the lake the cry was taken up.

Ten yards to go! Five!

At the building he fell to his knees beside the corrugated metal wall, gasping for breath. He pressed the open end of the ball of C4 against the metal.

The structure was between him and the mine, but he could hear a hue and cry going up still further away. The guards who were armed were, he knew, bunkered somewhere still farther down the lake, and they would be turning out now.

Harada prayed the fuses would burn. He also prayed they would burn properly at the advertised fifteen seconds a foot. Sometimes they had a nasty way of burning faster.

He pulled one igniter. It sputtered and died. He pulled

another. Ignition! The tiny curl of smoke and bead of orange flame were a comfort. He pulled the third igniter, and it, too, flared. Two out of three was better than he'd expected.

Get away!

He started to run as fast as his laboring lungs and tired muscles would alow. Darkness and the rocks conspired against him. He stumbled and sprawled, grazing his knees and hands. No matter, he told himself. Ignore it. He scrambled to his feet, the shouting behind him driving him on.

His lungs seemed about to burst, and his throat was dry, constricted. Age and terror were joined against him. The hundred yards seemed like a hundred miles. Could he find his hiding place? The AKM?

White lights suddenly flashed on all around. The spotlights! There was the harsh rip of automatic rifle fire. Bullets snapped past him, ricocheting against the rocks.

Here!

He dived for cover behind the ferns and rocks, oblivious to the sharp stones beneath him. As he did, he felt a hammer blow on the calf of his leg. He hit the ground, rolling, grabbed the rifle, switched it to fire, and let loose a long random burst toward his pursuers.

Then he fell back behind the rocks, fighting for breath. Blood pounded in his temples. Was this what it was like to strangle? The livid face of the young Cuban scout crossed his mind and disappeared as more bullets cracked and hummed around his cover.

He knew they would be hugging the ground, taking cover behind the engine house. He had bought a little time.

Quickly, he inspected his leg. There was a deep, straight gouge across the flesh, but it was not serious. He tore a strip of his shirt and made a compress, then strapped it tight with his belt.

Again he pushed the AKM through the ferns and fired a long burst in the general direction of Cinabre. The act seemed to require an inordinate amount of concentration. Indeed, he felt a kind of lassitude now, the false comfort of one

[146]

danger that is slightly less than another, like a pain that has lessened.

The fuses!

He pressed the AKM trigger again, not even looking toward Cinabre. Anything to make them keep their heads down, stay on their own side of the engine house.

How long would the damn fuses smolder? His thoughts blurred. What had he cut? One-minute lengths? Two?

Time seemed to stop. A montage of sharp, bright images unreeled in Harada's mind. They blurred. Then unconsciousness overcame him.

III

When the warning horns ceased, Karuchkin had emerged from his heavily shielded control room near the reactor to supervise the restoration of the tram in its underwater housing. He carried a clipboard with a checklist.

"How many kilos in this lot?" he asked a technician.

"Twenty-one, sir."

Karuchkin noted the number and the date on an account sheet. Mentally, he computed the value, one of his favorite exercises. If the price of gold were a hundred and fifty U.S. dollars per ounce, this lot would be worth more than a hundred and ten thousand dollars. Not a bad day's work. Now, if Desceau could only get the stuff to Texas for refining . . .

The thought of Texas reminded him for some reason of that strange prisoner in the tool cage. What had that encounter meant? Whatever else it was, it was a certain threat.

"You may open the corridor door now," he directed a guard.

Karuchkin looked up at the vast domed latticework of concrete above him, then let his eyes fall and linger on the glittering pool housing the reactor. It was a remarkable technical feat under these circumstances.

Winches were hauling the tram back down its tracks toward an inclined ramp that led, in turn, to the edge of the reactor. There the wheeled car fitted snugly to await its fresh cargo of gold-and-mercury amalgam.

Yes, he thought, this is a marvel, but one that the world would not know. Not yet. In ten years, twenty, the story might be revealed. Unless, of course, there was a defector . . . or the KGB . . .

The technician slid back the heavy bar of the steel door to the tool corridor and started to swing the door open.

In that instant the heavy door slammed into him and knocked him flat on his back. The white-haired man leaped out and covered them with an automatic rifle.

The scientist froze.

"Karuchkin!" Wolfram shouted. "Tell your guards to back away. We're going down the tunnel."

All of the physicist's fears converged suddenly on his reactor, his controls. *"Don't Shoot! Anyone!"* he cried.

A surprised guard near the exit corridor let his rifle muzzle dip uncertainly. The sounds of more guards approaching echoed down the main tunnel.

Wolfram came up beside him. "Tell 'em, Karuchkin. We're going out."

"They won't obey me. I'm not their commander."

"They won't shoot you, either. You're too valuable."

"Don't count on that. They are fools."

Wolfram fired a three-round burst at the tunnel ceiling over the guards' heads. A light shattered and went out. "Hey!" he shouted in Spanish. "We're coming down the tunnel. You fire at me and you'll hit your scientist!"

An answering shot zipped overhead. "You don't get past us, gringo," a soldier shouted. "Put down your rifle."

Wolfram hooked his hand into the back of Karuchkin's trousers belt and put the scientist between himself and the guards, who now had stopped and were kneeling, rifles up.

"Don't fire," Karuchkin called to them. "You might damage the equipment."

"And if you shoot me, you have to shoot your scientist," said Wolfram. "Colonel Guiteras won't like that. And Harry Desceau won't like it. He'll eat you for breakfast."

There was a muttered command in Spanish. The guards' rifles came down from their shoulders. "It's a standoff!" yelled the sergeant in command. "*We* can wait." He laughed out loud. "Guiteras will not be back until tomorrow. You will get very tired, gringo."

At that moment the lights dimmed, then went out. The chamber became pitch-black. From down the corridor to the outside came the compressive thud of an explosion.

"What happened?" Karuchkin demanded.

"What I was waiting for, Doctor. Now we exit through the dark. Keep your mouth shut. Come on." He pressed the scientist ahead of him. The path was engraved on his mind, and he walked it as if in daylight.

Guards called to each other in the darkness.

But almost as quickly as the main lights had faded, a dim red glow appeared, then brightened somewhat.

"*Damn!*" snarled Wolfram. This was unexpected.

Karuchkin looked over his shoulder at the other man. "The emergency lighting system, of course. Do you think we would stake our whole operation on the functioning of one large diesel? We have another, a small one, down another corridor. You didn't count on that, did you?"

"No."

Wolfram heard the sergeant's voice. "Give it up, gringo. You're not going anywhere."

Wolfram, still clutching Karuchkin's belt, began backing away.

"What are you doing?"

"We're going up that metal stairway to the top of the dome."

"You're an idiot. There's no way out up there."

"On the contrary, I think there is."

"I tell you, there isn't. It's a dead end. We use those stairs

[149]

to service our electrical systems in the dome. The only thing above that is the mountain."

"In fact," Wolfram replied, "I have something else in mind. Do you swim, Doctor?"

"You're mad."

The dim red light provided barely enough illumination to guide them around the reactor pool to the metal scaffolding that supported the stairs. The steps were steep, broken every twenty feet by railed landings leading to catwalks.

They began to climb backward.

"Did your people sabotage the engine house?"

"Certainly." A thought suddenly occurred to Wolfram. "Will the power loss affect your reactor?"

"The reactor generates its own power. The pool lights, of course, are on the main and emergency power systems. And then, we will not be able to empty our tram tomorrow unless a hand system is worked out. It would be very dangerous."

"It'll probably be academic," Wolfram muttered.

"Why?"

Wolfram did not answer.

Below them the red lights in and above the pool glowed like cats' eyes in the softer glow of the reactor's beta radiation. Guards edged forward in the shadows, rifles at the ready.

"Up we go, Doctor," said Wolfram. "We'll have a long night. Tell me about your marvelous machine."

Chapter Sixteen

I

The partially darkened room shivered, and Desceau heard the sound of a door opening. He turned to peer into the shadows. "Who is it?"

"Corporal Ortiz, sir."

"What is it?"

"There is an important radio message from Cinabre, sir."

"What now?"

"There has been an attack. The engine house has been exploded and the main power supply is out."

"*What?*"

"There has been an attack. . . ."

"I heard *that!* Where were the guards?"

The guard looked at his penciled notes. "The attack occurred just after the mine cart was emptied into the lake, just about the time the spotlights were to be turned on. The guards had gone to the bunker. But also there are not so many there because a number went on patrol with Colonel Guiteras."

"Casualties?"

"Three guards were exploded with the engine, sir."

"Did they get any of the attackers?"

"Our survivors say they are sure they got several, but the killed and wounded were dragged away into the jungle."

"Did they pursue?"

"The men believe there will be another attack before daylight. They have secured themselves in the bunker, and the ones inside the mine are staying there. The mine entrance is well covered."

"How did they get this radio message without power?"

"Some of the men carried the portable equipment up on the mountain and hooked it into the main antenna."

"They're lucky these attackers didn't knock out the antenna." He wondered about that. Trained guerrillas would have thought of the antenna first. Without communications their target would have been deaf and dumb, as well as blind in the darkness.

"Did they identify the attackers?"

"The guards insist it was guerrillas, sir. They saw Indians, especially the one who ran in and put explosives by the engine house. And there was much automatic rifle fire. At least a platoon."

Desceau discounted that information. He knew that in fire fights, the enemy was always multiplied by fear, darkness, and stupidity. He rubbed his chin thoughtfully. "How many men do we have out there now?"

"Colonel Guiteras and his patrol are ten. Three are dead."

"Leaving how many at Cinabre?"

"Six in the bunker and five inside the mine. Eleven."

Desceau thought of Wolfram. Had this been some kind of rescue attempt? How could his people know he was a prisoner?

"Any word from inside the mine?"

"No word, sir. But they are safe. No guerrillas got to the mine."

"The guards inside have the doctor and his three people with them. No help there . . ."

"What are your orders, sir?"

"Let me think a minute."

He wondered again about Firebird. Even with Wolfram a prisoner, there were four or five of them. But would they carry out an armed attack on Cinabre? It seemed out of character. He knew they went unarmed. That had been checked. Besides, Guiteras's patrol was somewhere between them and Cinabre, assuming they were at the high lake.

Perhaps the attack had been carried out by guerrillas. Could Firebird have made an arrangement with the guerrillas after all? It was plausible. If guerrillas continued to harass Cinabre, their activities would make it difficult for Cinabre to operate. Another big mineral company could then offer to buy Cinabre out.

Sure! That's the way it was done all the time. Why else would they use Indians and automatic weapons? The Firebird people said themselves that they were working for a big outfit. *They* wouldn't do the dirty work, but they could hire guerrillas to do it for them.

"Clever," Desceau muttered to himself. "Very clever."

"Sir?"

"Never mind," Desceau snapped. "These are your orders. Radio the men at Cinabre to sit tight. Tell them I am personally bringing up reinforcements. Then round up every man you can get. We have guns here for fifteen, but there are more at Cinabre. Get the men here in an hour. From here we will take the trucks to Atranango, and from there by foot to Cinabre."

"Tonight, sir?"

"*Tonight!*"

II

When awareness returned, Harada did not know how long he had been out. It could have been minutes or hours. Painfully, cautiously, he raised himself up on his elbow to look behind the shelter of the rocks.

Where the engine house had been there was now only a jagged central mass surrounded by blackened debris. Illumination came from small, guttering fires of diesel fuel. The blast must have been shattering, Harada thought. The hundred yards between him and the explosion had been barely enough.

He checked the compress over his throbbing wound. There was little bleeding. The ache along the bullet's path was more tolerable than the sting of perspiration rolling over his many abrasions.

He lifted himself up again to make a more careful survey of the terrain. The plan had been for Wolfram to use the sudden cover of blackness inside the mine to make his getaway. At the mine entrance, he was to turn left and, by the light of the burning oil, make his way to Harada. Then the two of them would have hidden in the jungle until . . .

In retrospect, it was a weak plan, for it was predicated on too many variables. True, Wolfram had done precisely this kind of thing on other occasions and bluffed it through. But tonight's scheme was not up to any of Wolfram's standards of acceptable risk. Indeed, thought Harada, the risk he had taken in accepting the invitation inside Cinabre would have to be graded unacceptable on all counts. It had been desperate; worse, it had added to the risk all the rest of them had to take.

Harada felt no particular anger about any of this. His analysis, considering the circumstances, was objective. Had the plan succeeded, he probably would have thought about it the same way. But now it was quite clear that the scheme had failed.

Wolfram had not emerged from the mine.

Harada stared at his leg. There was no way he could cover the yards between here and Cinabre. It would be difficult enough scrambling up to high ground when the flood came.

That brought his thoughts back to Wolfram.

Very likely, Wolfram was dead. At the very least, he was prisoner in a chamber that soon would be flooded. And Wolfram would drown.

III

It was nearly midnight when the three-truck convoy rumbled through the deserted plaza of Chichicastenango, past the brooding church, and on out the unpaved road to Atranango. The night was bright, cold, and very clear.

Desceau, an AKM clamped upright between his knees, rode beside the driver in the lead truck. He wore a bush jacket over a thick sweater, and a wool scarf around his neck. The temperature was close to freezing and the dry highland air sharpened the cold. Over his jacket, Desceau wore a regulation Cuban-Soviet belt and harness with ammunition pouches, canteen, and first-aid kit.

The three trucks carried an assortment of seventeen Cinabre guards and Indian workers recruited for the mission with a promise of triple pay. Desceau had no illusions about the quality of his troops.

At the edge of the tiny village of Atranango they stopped beside corrals that sheltered the Cinabre mules.

Desceau dismounted stiffly. "Ortiz!" he shouted.

The corporal climbed out of the cab of the second truck. "Sir?"

"Tell the men to fall out and gather around me."

Shortly, Desceau stood within a circle of his motley troops. Some wore the Cuban-style fatigues of the Cinabre guards. Others wore Indian tunics and serapes belted down by ammunition harness and pouches. All held their rifles as they might canes or fishing poles. It was an incredibly unmilitary-looking group, thought Desceau. He tried to focus on them in the pale light of the moon.

"From here it is fifty kilometers to Cinabre. Some of you have walked it before with the mules. But this time we are in a hurry, so we will ride the mules."

Behind him one of the animals brayed.

"It will be a long trip," Desceau continued. "We will follow the regular Cinabre trail along the river valley. When we draw near to the Cinabre lake, we will deploy for action and advance to the mine. The trail is not difficult, but darkness will slow us. We should be at Cinabre in ten or eleven hours. By noon at the latest. I will be at the head of the column with the guide. Corporal Ortiz will be with the rear guard. Keep the line well closed up, understand? We do not expect trouble on this trail, but we take no chances. Are there questions?"

There were none.

"Very well. Ortiz, wake up the mule drivers to help us saddle up."

An hour later, they all were clopping along the trail to Cinabre, legs dangling from improvised saddles of blankets and rope.

Chapter Seventeen

I

All things considered, it had been a miserable night for Kinsey. The lake's pervasive mist had seeped into his bones, and low temperatures aggravated the chill. Every stone around him poked a rib or vertebra. Even when, mercifully, he dozed off, frequent tremors jarred him awake again.

He sat up, shivering, and tugged his blanket tighter around his shoulders. The sky was brightening. He glanced at his watch. Five fifteen. Sunrise would be at five forty-one.

He edged forward and peered over the natural ramparts. It was still quite dark in the gorge below. There were no lights. Mist from the lake rolled over the dam like a cloud of smoke and wafted in long streamers into the dark valley.

Kinsey retreated from the brink to a group of boulders and took a chocolate bar from his jacket pocket. He nibbled the bar slowly, savoring each fragment. It was a small comfort, he thought, but a lousy breakfast.

A minute later he heard a rattle of stones nearby and a hoarse whisper.

"Kinsey?"

"Here."

Magraw's black shape separated from the shadows and crawled over to him. Over his shoulder he wore a musette bag containing a large spool of insulated wire and a hand generator that could trigger electrically fired detonators.

"How did it go?"

"Cold, wet, dark, lumpy . . ."

"I mean the Cinabre patrol."

"They settled down. I just hope they were as miserable."

"Do you think they turned back?"

"Doubt it."

Magraw produced binoculars. "Maybe we can pick them up with these."

"It's still dark down there."

Magraw twisted around and squinted at the sky. "I'll switch on the seismic system around sunup. Then all we have to do is wait for Mother Nature to do her thing."

Kinsey took the binoculars and edged forward again. He peered down into the gorge.

"See anything?"

"One sentry, sitting on a rock. The others must be under cover."

Magraw moved up beside him. "Let me see."

Kinsey passed the glasses to him.

Magraw watched for a minute or two. "I think I can make out some others. They're beginning to move around." He shifted position. "I count six, seven . . ."

"Don't get too close to the edge. They might see you."

Magraw rolled onto his elbows, glasses up. He could see the Cinabre men clearly now. They were on their feet, buckling up their equipment. They seemed to be wading in clouds of mist. "I think they're going to make their move."

A faint tremor dislodged stones somewhere down the moraine. They rattled down into the gorge.

"Watch it," said Kinsey.

Magraw saw faces turning his way. He could not make out their features in the mist and shadow. The figures seemed to be organizing themselves into a line. He shifted again, trying to bring the abstractions into focus. One of the shapes raised an arm toward him.

"Oh, oh." Magraw recoiled back behind the parapet.

"What's the matter?"

[158]

"I think one of them spotted my glasses."

"We're silhouetted against the sky up here."

"Damn," Magraw muttered. "Now they'll know we're here and come up." He passed the binoculars to Kinsey. "Take a look, but keep your head down."

The flier snaked forward and focused the binoculars on the activity below. Several were staring up at the dam. Others were looking elsewhere. Quickly, he backed away again.

"If those guys saw you, they don't seem too excited," he said. "But we'd better set the detonators, anyway."

"Right. I'll take care of that. You get back to the helicopter and stand by. I'll watch the Cinabres awhile, then switch on the gear."

"How long will it take them to get up here?"

"Depends how many rocks I roll down. Twenty minutes, maybe."

"Not much time. Don't cut it too thin."

Magraw chuckled. *"Thin?* The word isn't in my vocabulary."

Kinsey slapped him on the shoulder and slid away.

The jagged rim of the dam was brightening perceptibly. Magraw watched Kinsey go, then turned back to observe the Cinabre patrol through the binoculars. It was light enough now for them not to use their lanterns as they threaded their way through the clutter of boulders. He did another head count. There were nine of them, each carrying an AKM.

Before long the patrol reached the steeper base of the high dam. There the file closed into a group, presumably, thought Magraw, to plan their ascent.

He did some planning of his own. Kinsey would need plenty of light to carry his mission to Gamma lake. The approach of the Cinabre patrol was putting a time squeeze on that. He wondered whether they had seen him before, or had the arm waving been coincidental? Would they move slower or faster if they knew an adversary was above them? How would he react under those circumstances?

"Cautiously," he said to himself. "*Very* cautiously."

Caution would cost the patrol time. Time was what Firebird needed. An extra hour would do it.

He glanced at his watch. It was now five thirty-nine. Sunup would come in two minutes, but the long mountain shadows would linger well into morning.

Once again he edged up to the parapet and scanned with the glasses. A small advance guard had already started climbing. The rest stood around casually, smoking.

At the rate the early starters were moving, the climb would not take very long. The general angle of the palisade ranged from about forty-five degrees in the lower half to sixty degrees in the upper half, but the climbing was like moving up a staircase with five- or six-foot risers and plenty of hand- and footholds. A comfortable morning's exercise for a healthy man.

Too comfortable, Magraw decided. He would have to do something about it.

Slowly he worked a large rock from its matrix, then carried it in a crouch to the edge of the moraine. He didn't care about—in fact, invited—their seeing him. For a moment he stood there, staring into the gorge below. None of them was looking his way.

Struggling a little, he hoisted the thirty-pound rock high over his head, then heaved it out as far as he could. It caught the light as it fell, then cracked into boulders and broke into fist-size fragments that rained down on the party far below.

He heard shouts and watched as the advance party scrambled back down over the boulders and ran for cover. He picked up another rock, smaller this time, and hurled it after them. Several other members of the patrol dropped to a kneeling position, cocking their rifles. Magraw ducked as bullets snapped overhead, followed an instant later by the ripping sound of automatic rifle fire. They were aiming far too high.

They had gotten his message, in any case. Now it was time to go.

Scrambling awkwardly on hands and knees, he moved back across the top of the moraine to a place where he could stand up out of the patrol's field of fire. Once he reached the seismic equipment, nestled behind a large slab, he took Wolfram's typed checklist out of his pocket and went through the drill. As always, there were multiple sets of equipment. Before switching it on, he removed the large spool of insulated wire from his musette bag, stripped the insulation with his wire cutters, and connected the ends to screw terminals on the equipment.

Next came the ticklish part. He had to turn on each of the tremor-sensitive devices, then pray that an earthquake didn't occur at the same instant he tried to make his getaway.

The black man wiped his hands carefully on his handkerchief, then flicked the switches in the sequence indicated on his checklist. The little read Active lights winked on. The dial readings said all of the circuits were clear, none losing power.

Now to get away before nature reacted. Magraw jogged as fast as his thick legs could move him toward the main lakeshore. Insulated wire unreeled behind him from the big spool, a thin, almost invisible wake.

II

Hot brass cartridge cases littered the rocks. The moist air was suffused with the acrid odor of cordite. Guiteras emerged from cover. "Cease fire!" he ordered.

The appearance of the figure above, like some mountain monster, had been a shock. Even more stunning had been the sight and sound of rocks bounding like slow-motion cannonballs directly at them.

Their answering fire had sent the figure back behind the rim of the dam, but he probably was still there, ready to heave another skull-crushing stone at them. For the moment, however, there was silence.

"Fall in!" Guiteras commanded.

[161]

Reluctantly, his men reemerged from sheltering boulders.

Guiteras jabbed his finger at several of them. "You! You! You! Take positions and give us covering fire as we go up."

"We're going *up,* sir?" the sergeant asked incredulously.

"Yes, Sergeant, we are going up. Will your stomach stand the altitude?"

The sergeant stiffened to attention. "Ready, sir!"

Guiteras unbuckled his pack and let it drop. He was breathing too fast, he knew, and he was sweating from fear, not heat. "I will lead the advance party. Two men will go up with me. Rifles and ammunition only. Sergeant, you and the others will follow behind us by two to three hundred yards."

Guiteras looked around to make certain the three riflemen he had singled out were in position. "Shoot at anything that moves up there, but between targets I want you to maintain a suppressive fire, you understand. Keep the devils' heads down."

"Do you think they are armed, Colonel?" asked the sergeant.

The two men selected to go with Guiteras shed their packs and slung their rifles across their backs. As they began the ascent, the heavy thud of AKMs sounded sporadically behind them.

III

Kinsey was waiting for him where the moraine smoothed out somewhat into a moss-shrouded shoreline. Magraw's jog slowed to a stagger.

"Oh, man, this altitude kills me." He leaned on Kinsey's arm for support as they began to walk slowly toward the helicopter several hundred yards away. "What are you doing here? You were supposed to get on back to the chopper."

"I heard the shooting and came back. What touched them off?"

Magraw grinned. "I did. I figured if they saw somebody topside, they'd have to slow down."

The muffled popping of random shots echoed from the gorge.

"If that Colonel Guiteras has read the book, he's got a party coming up under covering fire. That shooting's supposed to make me quit throwing rocks at them."

"It's working."

"But believe me, those boys are taking some time to look up and see what might be coming down."

"Did those detonators turn on the way they were supposed to?"

Magraw nodded. "The real question is, Will they work?"

"What if they don't?"

Magraw patted his musette bag with its trail of wire. "That's when we have to use this." He pulled the wire spool from the bag. Only a few feet remained, attached to the black hand generator.

"Let's find a concealed place and hook this up. The wire's running out."

They started as the ground shuddered underfoot.

"We may not have a chance to hook it up," said Kinsey. "How much of a quake does this seismic gear need to work it?"

"Something on the order of a Richter Scale Three." Magraw dropped to his knees behind a shelf of rock and began connecting the wire to the generator terminals.

"That could take hours!" Kinsey exclaimed. "Meanwhile, Harada and Wolfram are scrambling around down by Cinabre, trying to dodge patrols or God knows what."

"We hope." Magraw glanced at Kinsey. "I'm going to stay behind with this thing. Just in case those Cinabre boys get up the hill. I wouldn't want to chance their getting between me and the generator. Or worse, they might cut off the whole works at the seismic gear."

"Why don't we just fire it now?" Kinsey said with some

exasperation. "Why wait for some damn earthquake when armed men are creeping up on us? There's enough C4 out there. . . ."

Magraw shook his head. "Let's do what the man says. I read through the calculations and the thing is only going to work right with a tremor."

"Thome says the calculations are wrong."

"No, Thome said they're 'questionable.' "

The crackle of small-arms fire was heard again.

"You better get going," Magraw told Kinsey. "The Cinabres should be here in about ten minutes."

Kinsey glowered at him. "This was the plan all the time, wasn't it? You stay behind and play Horatio-at-the-bridge in case Mother Nature doesn't come through. A real live hero!"

"Cut it out!" Magraw growled. "I'll be all right. I've got both concealment and cover here. If worse comes to worst, I'll hide out in the woods. You can come back for me later in the week. That patrol won't hang around forever."

Kinsey shook his head. "You know, this is the most catch-as-catch-can operation Wolfram ever suckered himself—and us—into. I get the feeling things are coming unglued. Even the detonator wire runs short. That's bad planning."

"Don't count Wolfram out. Things change, and he's got to fight every round as it comes up. He's rolling with the punches."

"But is he landing any?"

Magraw pointed at the dam. "We've got one big one right there."

"If it works."

IV

Back at the helicopter, Kinsey explained about Magraw.

"But will he be safe there, that close to the dam?" asked Juanita. "And what if the Cinabre shooters see him?"

"He'll be okay," Kinsey replied. He didn't believe it himself.

Thome stared out at the lake. "There will be only three of us, then." Like Juanita, he was already dressed in an underwater suit, ready to hook up equipment.

"Wrong," said Kinsey. "Wolfram and Harada are already at Cinabre. They're your backup. After I drop you two, I'll come back up here, collect Magraw, give you folks enough time to get in and out of the mine, then pick you all up. Simple."

"Nonsense!" snapped Thome. "This whole thing is a disaster. . . ."

"That's enough!" Kinsey did not need to be reminded of his own misgivings.

The flier got a pair of binoculars from the helicopter and surveyed the lake rim. Nothing. He scanned shoreward until he could pick out Magraw huddled in some foliage behind his rock. Then, near the lake outfall, his glasses picked up a movement. "Oh, oh. Here they come."

"Cinabre!" Juanita whispered.

Kinsey refocused the glasses. "One man up. Now two. Three."

"Earthquake!" Juanita implored. *"Por favor!"*

"Shouldn't we warm up the engines or something, Kinsey?" Thome demanded. "Those people are within rifle range."

Kinsey nodded and handed the glasses to Juanita. He climbed up into the aircraft, and an instant later, the turbines began to whine.

At the edge of the dam Juanita could see the three men looking their way. One of them motioned with his hands, the other two unslung their rifles.

"Get down!" she shouted to Thome, shoving him at the same time. An instant later there was the slap-slap of bullets cutting through foliage. The riflemen were way off the mark. Accuracy would be impossible at such a range. Still, an unlucky shot might find one of them.

[165]

"Get inside!" she yelled at Thome.

With unusual agility he vaulted into the helicopter, followed by the woman. A bullet pinged against the fuselage.

"Don't worry," Kinsey yelled to them over the engines. "At this range those 7.62-millimeter slugs don't have any more zip than a pebble."

The aircraft was quivering in synchronization with its engines. But then, oddly, it began to sway from side to side, as if pulled by invisible wires.

"Look!" Juanita shouted.

The far-off trio of riflemen appeared to be caught in a violent gust of wind that was blowing them off their feet. They dropped their rifles. Two of them fell to their hands and knees, while the third staggered drunkenly from side to side.

"Earthquake!"

At that moment the placid lake blossomed with great white surges of froth where the outfall was.

"The charges fired!"

Almost as if in slow motion, the visible edges of the moraine, with the three men clinging to them, slid sideways, then, like a raft of logs, moved forward, turned, and disappeared.

A great V, smooth and gleaming, sliced into the edge of the lake where the top of the dam had been. Slowly, the depression filled in again as the surface of the lake caught up with gravity and the line was restored.

The only sign of movement to be seen now through the glasses was a broad stripe of bubbles streaking like arrows toward the void on the other side of what remained of the dam. They were the only hint that a vast mountain of water was crashing through the gorge below.

Chapter Eighteen

I

At sunrise, Harada awoke. For a minute he lay still, eyes open, listening to the birds.

During the night, after the fuel fires had finally burned out, he had limped, crawled, and clawed his way through the darkness up the steep side of the ridge that dominated the western edge of Cinabre's lake, and secured himself in a cove of boulders and brush.

Sleep had been fitful. Time and again the trembling of the mountain—or the painful leg wound—had awakened him.

Harada elbowed himself carefully up out of his prone position until he leaned against a rocky outcropping. Gently, he untied the compress on his leg and peeled it away to expose the wound. Fresh blood oozed through a crust of dirt and dried blood, but otherwise it wasn't too bad.

He tore another strip from his tunic and made a new compress, put it on the wound, and strapped it tight, wincing against the sharp needle of pain.

That done, he removed the magazine from the automatic rifle, stripped the cartridges from it, and counted them. Ten. That was some reassurance. He was not totally helpless.

He squinted at the sun, just now slicing through a cut in the eastern ridge, and wondered about the others. The plan, he knew, was for the explosives to be triggered with the first sharp tremor after dawn. It could already have happened.

Using the AKM as a crutch, he heaved himself up to look

beyond the rocks that sheltered him, a good sixty or seventy feet above the lake's waterline. Almost directly below him he could see the blackened junk of the blast, human and mechanical.

The angle of the slope cut off his view of the Cinabre entrance, but much farther down the lake, where the ridgeline curved eastward to close in the end of the valley, he could see the bunker. The snout of a machine gun poked from one of the gun ports. A narrow sandbagged trench led to a sally port.

There was no movement anywhere.

In the opposite direction, on the northern rim of the lake, the ridgeline also closed, forming a modest gorge of rapids and jungle leading back to the middle lake. There, too, all was still, silent, and dark.

The silence wouldn't last, he knew. Or would it?

Harada weighed the possibilities. The triggering business could misfire, of course. Guiteras and his men could have interdicted the others. Harada shook his head, discarding such demoralizing possibilities.

Once the dam was broken, how fast would the raging water travel the four miles or so to Gamma Lake? A mile a minute? Faster? Even as it came, it would seal the doom of Wolfram.

The ground seemed to tremble.

Or was that a vibration heard more than felt?

Now there was a fresh sound, like a small breeze through wind chimes, getting stronger.

Running water! Tumbling water!

Harada pulled himself up for a better view of the lake. Nothing was precisely discernible there. Yet the mist on the northern perimeter seemed to be swirling.

Now the swirling moved across the lake in microcosmic white tornadoes, slowly at first, then with more and more speed.

He looked out at the tops of the pier pilings in the lake,

suspended in the mist. The swirls approached, circled, caught and moved around them. Intently, he studied the edge of the mist where it faded into the shoreline.

There it was! Wavelets lapping inland, a rising tide.

The mist was swirling violently now, all over the lake. He could hear the waves slapping more and more loudly on the shore. The tide rose relentlessly. A tongue of water speared down a declivity between the pier and the mine entrance, then another and another, until they all joined and the whole area was inundated.

Harada could not see it, but he knew the water was beginning to flood the mine itself. In the blackness there, no one would know until it was too late. No one but Wolfram, of course—if he lived.

Still the waters rose. The waves, virtual breakers now, crashed against the rocks below. The mists were blown away now by the flood.

Harada looked back toward the middle lake. Where just minutes before there had been a silent, somber, half-lit jungle river there was now a white-capped race studded with broken trees and streaked with soil and stone.

Harada looked down toward the bunker, now half submerged. A figure at the sally port struggled against the current flowing down the trench. The man hurled himself along, barely making headway, until at last he was able to heave himself over the edge of the tumbling sandbags, scramble to his feet, run down the trench line, across the top of the bunker, and leap for the steep side of the ridge. He kicked his way upward until he found a shelf of rock that he followed to safety on high ground.

Another figure pressed out of the sally port, chest-deep in water. For an instant he held his own. Then the weight of the torrent hurled him back inside. The tide came up and the door was sealed.

Harada looked up above his own outpost. Could he make it higher? He and Wolfram had estimated that the explosives

[169]

would produce a twenty- to twenty-five-foot rise on Gamma lake. Already the flood was passing that level, and still the overriding tiers of water flowed across, followed by others without a letup.

Wolfram!

Harada knew he was gone beyond recall, doomed inside the black mountain, like the poor Cuban washed back to drown inside the bunker.

II

The trail from Atranango to Cinabre hugged the jungle-bound river valley as it ascended gently into the Sierra de Flan. It was a hot, dark tunnel through the rain forest. Throughout the steaming night, the mules had plodded nose-to-tail through the darkness, following the flicker of the guide's lantern. From time to time the men of Desceau's patrol walked, leading their animals, but always they kept moving.

By Desceau's estimate they had made good time. The trail was firm at this season, and the few streams they had forded were shallow. At 5:30 A.M. by his watch he had decided they were more than halfway to their objective. He kicked his mule and pulled up beside the guide.

"We will stop here for the men to eat."

The guide hauled up the lantern dangling on a rope to one side of the mule's belly and waved it slowly to and fro. A murmur of voices rippled down the column.

"Dismount! Rest!" Desceau shouted. "Tell Corporal Ortiz to come forward."

When Ortiz appeared a moment later, Desceau told him, "The guide and I will go ahead to reconnoiter."

"What can you see in this darkness?"

"Nothing. But the sun will be coming up soon. We will go up on the ridge where the visibility will be better." Desceau motioned the guide closer. "How far are we now from Cinabre?"

"Fifteen kilometers."

"*That* close? How do you know?"

"Each kilometer is marked by a pile of stones. Each five kilometers has two piles. We have just passed the seventh double pile."

"Better than I'd thought," Desceau muttered. To the guide, he said, "I want to find a place where we can go up the side of the mountain and see the Cinabre lake. Do you know such a place?"

"You have the twin glasses?"

Desceau patted his binoculars case.

"Then there is such a place. We must go up the trail two more kilometers, then go up." He pointed into the darkness toward the ridge hidden behind the jungle. "But the mules cannot go there."

"We'll walk." Desceau removed his canteen from its pouch and took a drink. "Ortiz," he said, "you and the others will sit tight here until I get back or send the guide to bring you up."

"Very well, sir."

"You can smoke and eat, but keep the lanterns out."

Desceau checked the chamber of his automatic rifle, and started up the trail, following the guide with the lantern. Despite the smothering humidity, they walked rapidly. Twenty minutes later, the guide stopped and pointed first to a cluster of moss-slicked rocks, and then to a place only he could see, above the rocks. Desceau nodded and gestured that they should move on.

On the other side of the jumbled boulders, they reached a thick stratum that angled upward, and began to climb. The muscles of Desceau's thighs and calves protested. Soon his heart was pounding against the strenuous work. He looked up. The umbrella of forest was behind them, and he could see the sky, already bright above them. A current of cool air wafted over them.

[171]

Still they plodded on. Just when Desceau thought he would have to stop the guide for a rest, the man stopped, blew out his now needless lantern, and put it down. "This the place."

Desceau advanced the last twenty feet and looked around. The sky in the east was day-bright now, but the sun hadn't quite moved above the eastern ridgeline. Nevertheless, the valley leading up to the Cinabre lake was open in front of him. The western ridge was more or less illuminated; the east, still black as night.

Desceau took his binoculars out of their case and surveyed the lake itself. It looked like a bowl of whipped cream, the mist floating out along the valley where it narrowed into the rapids and shallow waterfalls. The jungle was a gray-green belt along the bottom of the valley, completely concealing the trail and much of the river. The layers of foliage thinned as the slope steepened.

The jungle trail is a good approach, Desceau thought. Perfect concealment. Unfortunately, it could conceal the guerrillas as well. Furthermore, they undoubtedly knew the trail better than he did, and could probably pick the best spots for ambush.

He dismissed the Cinabre trail as an approach route. They would have to do it over the mountains.

"Is there a trail down this ridge into Cinabre?" he asked the guide.

"This trail go down the ridge over *top* of Cinabre." He pointed down the spine of the sierra.

"Is it a hard trail? Much climbing?"

"Rocky trail. Some up and down. No climbing with hands."

"Good." Desceau scanned the ridge. This was probably the same approach route the guerrillas had used. The angle of attack on the engine house jibed with the double-back of the trail. It would be nice to catch them at their own game.

"Go back and tell Ortiz to bring the men up," he said to the guide. "Tell him to pick two to take the mules back to Atranango. Understood?"

"*Claro.*"

Desceau waved him off, then ambled farther along the ridge path. On a high, flat rock he hauled himself up and took a position to study the valley. The shadow over the lake and shoreline was retreating perceptibly now as the sun moved higher. He focused his glasses on the long stretch of rapids and huge boulders where the overflow of the lake was choked into sluices by the two ridges.

It all seemed very remote and silent. But as he watched, the stream of undulating water through the rapids began suddenly to boil. Funny, he thought. He rested his elbows against his chest to steady the binoculars.

In an instant there seemed to be more water flowing around, up, and over the rocks. Then more. Then torrents. Plumes of spray shot violently into the air. He could almost hear the rush.

"Flash flood!" he exclaimed aloud.

He swept the glasses back down the valley until he found the approximate place where his men were resting under the canopy of forest. They would never see this coming, probably not even hear it until, in an instant, they would be up to their necks in a raging current, tangling in trees, drowning.

Helplessly, he watched as the tide plunged on down the valley, sweeping away whole chunks of forest before it.

"Cinabre!"

He spun around again to study the lake. Its mist was gone now and he could see the surface. It looked like a small sea in a storm, waves rolling and churning.

The lake was rising, there could be no mistaking that. The narrow gorge below was incapable of carrying off the flood as fast as it was coming in from . . . where?

Desceau's eyes narrowed. There was only one possibility.

[173]

The high lake. The dam. An earthquake, perhaps; a volcano. Or—a blast!

And then he saw it, a gleaming spot like some huge dragonfly. It was a helicopter skimming low over the lashing lake and down to the rapids. It seemed to stop in midair, then wheeled around the other way and disappeared from his view.

But not before he saw the orange symbol on its side.

Chapter Nineteen

I

Nothing was as it had been. Turbulent water had drowned every landmark Juanita had noted before. Through the middle of the lake a rolling current tossed jungle debris toward the outlet of the lake.

The helicopter hovered over the middle of the lake while she sought some sign of Wolfram and Harada. After a minute or two, she spotted some movement on the western slope.

"There!" she shouted at Kinsey.

The pilot looked, nodded his head, then leaned the aircraft that way. Twenty seconds later he had brought the aircraft over the ridge directly above Harada. He was alone.

The side of the ridge was too steep for Kinsey to put the craft down, but they had anticipated this. Juanita unfastened her seat harness, unlatched the door, and tossed out the Jacob's ladder.

Their diving gear was bundled inside two heavy rucksacks. Deftly, she shouldered hers, then helped Thorne into his. The scientist's eyes were glassy with fright. Exasperated, Juanita prodded him and pointed at the door, with the ladder dancing below.

"You first," she shouted above the helicopter sounds.

Thorne crawled to the door on his hands and knees and looked out at the harsh, hard ground some fifteen feet below. He looked back at her imploringly.

"Go!" She pointed at the opening.

Crablike, Thome hauled himself and the rucksack to the ladder, grasped the top rung, then fumbled with his feet for a purchase. She hoped to God he wouldn't lose his nerve and fall. It would crush him.

Finally, he was over the side, knuckles white as he clutched the rungs. His head descended below the door rim, eyes sinking past it like two expiring moons.

Quickly, she moved to the door and watched him go down. Then she swung over the side and began her own descent. This was the most frightening part of helicopter work. One always had the senseless fear that the craft would suddenly bolt into the sky, leaving one dangling at a thousand feet.

She was down. Pushing Thome out of the way, she dropped her rucksack, ran to the front of the craft, and waved her arms. Kinsey saw her, gave the thumbs-up sign, and, banking the helicopter out over the lake, headed back up the gorge.

Juanita turned to Harada. "Where's Wolfram?"

The Japanese shook his head slowly. "He never came out of the mine."

It took her a few seconds to assimilate the news. She turned and looked at the water lapping just below them, wild and murky. Strangely, she felt no pang of remorse; she knew it would come later. Right now she was too keyed up.

She turned back to Harada. "What do you think?"

"There is no chance for him." He shifted uncomfortably, and, for the first time, she noticed his leg.

"You're injured."

"A bullet graze. Not so much serious as aggravating. But it limits my help."

"God, this is awful!" Thome exclaimed, his face reflecting desperation. "They could be all around us. Guerrillas."

Pointing toward the lake, Harada laughed shortly. "They're gone."

"Get your equipment on," Juanita ordered.

[176]

Thome gasped. "You're not going through with this! I've never seen more treacherous water."

"I have," Juanita said firmly. "Get your equipment on."

Thome lowered his rucksack and began to unpack the tanks, mask, fins, weight belt, writing gear, and a large underwater lantern.

Juanita did the same. As she worked, she asked Harada, "How did it go, otherwise?"

"Rather as planned. I'm afraid I'm a little slower these days, and the Cinabre reaction was a little quicker." He nodded ruefully at his injury.

"The Cinabre patrol was coming up the dam when . . . did you meet them yesterday?"

"Yes. Colonel Guiteras was leading them."

"They didn't try to stop you?"

"They tried." The look on Harada's face stopped Juanita from asking further questions. Instead, she double-checked Thome's breathing apparatus and tanks, then did the same for herself.

"All right," she said quietly, "we are going in now. Do you have your writing equipment?"

Hands shaking, he checked a canvas pouch attached to his weight belt. It held wax crayons and plastic writing tablets. "I'm prepared."

Juanita anchored a rope around a boulder, then tossed the end down the slope into the thrashing water to aid them in getting up and down. Grasping the rope, she began to slide and leap down to the surface of the lake, her fins slapping the rocks. In the water she gripped a shelf of stone and called back.

"All right, Dr. Thome. Down you come."

The physicist gripped the rope the way he had seen her do it, and flapped downward.

In the water, crosscurrents pushed them this way and that while they adjusted their face masks and regulators. But once they pushed off, they found that the current along the jagged shoreline was weak, tugging them directly toward the Cinabre mine area.

The two of them moved along the surface, Juanita leading, until they had covered about a hundred yards, to a point approximately over the mouth of the mine. She turned and gestured to Thome to follow her into a dive, switched on the lantern snapped onto harness cleats at her chest, and went under.

The turbidity wasn't as bad as it had seemed from the surface. Fortunately for the divers, the flood had come down over a rocky gorge, not bottomland.

She kicked straight down, following the steep angle of the ridge until she came to the tarmac that had been the work level outside the opening of the Cinabre mine area. There she looked back. Thome was flailing along in her wake of bubbles. He swims like Kinsey, she thought, all waving legs and inadequate thrust. If only he can hold out until we can haul him back to safety.

When he came up beside her, the two of them shone the beams of their lanterns systematically in different directions, looking for orientation points or the mine opening. Juanita's beam picked up the glint of tracks leading from the former pier. She followed them back with her light to the black hole of the mine opening itself. She nudged Thome's arm. The light was getting better all the time. The deep blue was fading to blue-green. Rays of sunlight illuminated the dancing grains of sediment in clear, bright stripes.

She kicked toward the ominous mine opening, Thome trailing along behind her like a pilot fish. At the entry she stopped and settled to test the current. It was still heading into the shaft, but it was not strong, which meant that there were empty chambers, still filling.

Beside her, Thome cast his light down the silent tunnel. The rays evaporated in blackness. He turned to her. The blue eyes were less frightened now, she noted. They seemed to be asking a question. In response, she pointed down the tunnel.

[178]

Reluctantly, he churned ahead. It was his turn to lead now, to find the reactor, get the information about the neutron reflectors, or whatever, and get out.

It seemed as if they were swimming into a well, though, in fact, they were moving horizontally. Soon the tubular walls of the tunnel opened out into a vast, black space. Thome moved toward it, but stopped suddenly at the brim of the tunnel, arms pumping in sudden panic. Quickly, she pulled up beside him.

A drowned Cuban, mouth agape, eyes accusing, stared at them. The corpse floated like a balloon at the end of its rifle sling, snagged on a pipe elbow.

Juanita pulled past Thome. Behind his mask his eyes rolled. She couldn't let him panic now. She clenched her fist, punched her knuckles smartly into his thin biceps, and briskly motioned him ahead again.

They came now to a maze of concrete beams. Just ahead of them the water glowed with a pale lavender aura, almost a phosphorescence. Juanita had seen this color before, glowing around some of the mercury/gold tubes that had been dumped into the lake.

Thome caught her arm. He knew that the aura was the so-called Cerenkov effect, caused by beta radiation from a nuclear reactor that is absorbed by water molecules. He took out a crayon and pad from his pouch and wrote the word reactor on it. He pointed up and made a swimming motion.

Juanita nodded that she understood. They swam to a point above the reactor to look down into it through the glowing, illuminating water. Soon the whole incredible piece of equipment was defined in its own light. Juanita glanced at Thome, who had deposited himself on a crossbeam, already sketching the layout, making notations. Thome's usually perplexed eyes were narrowed and intent on their work. Whatever frights he had suffered, he had forgotten them in his absorption with this technical problem.

Juanita took a perch beside him and cast the beam of her

lantern around the massive latticework of concrete. This was unquestionably a large chamber, heavily protected against the recurring earthquakes. The reactor was at least twenty or thirty feet below them. It was difficult to tell in the refracting water. The chamber stretched upward into darkness. She looked up, trying to gauge its possible height. Did the water level abut the ceiling, or . . . ?

What was that? A light above?

She touched Thome's arm and pointed upward. Irritated at being diverted from his problem, Thome glanced that way. For a moment there was nothing. Then there was a wink. The winking continued in the familiar SOS sequence. She turned off her lantern.

Thome's eyes questioned hers. She took the crayon from him and wrote "Wait here, I check" on his tablet. He nodded.

Hand over hand, she pulled her way along the beams in the direction of the winking light. This would take some care, for she couldn't go popping up in the sights of some Cinabre rifle. On the other hand, what was she to do if there were Cuban survivors there? Duck down again, leave them to die, possibly.

Of course, she knew, the waters would eventually subside. But how could anyone be sure? The chamber might be flooded forever. Or, even if the water subsided, it might still seal the tunnel exit.

The light, stronger to her eye now, came from one side of the chamber. She pulled that way, around and through the patterns of beams, and broke through the unseen surface.

The light turned on full beam and flashed into her face, blinding her before she could duck back down to safety. Voices reverberated eerily through the closed chamber, the domed roof above projecting them back from all around.

"Over here."

Despite the distortions, that tone was unmistakable.

Dodging along the surface around the superstructure, she

swam into the light. Moments later, she collided with a column of steel steps leading up to a platform a short distance above. She could make out two shapes illuminated by light reflected from the water.

"What took you so long?"

It was Wolfram.

Chapter Twenty

I

Wolfram, an AKM slung across his back, came down the steps and helped her out of the water. "Welcome to Cinabre."

She leaned back and rested her tanks against the steel railing before removing her mouthpiece and pushing her face mask up on her forehead.

"We thought we had lost you, Hugo."

"I thought so, too. But the water finally stopped rising. Our earthquake demolition worked better than I planned."

She smiled. "I'm glad you're all right. It wouldn't be the same without you."

"Especially for me," he said dryly.

She pointed at the other figure. "Who is that?"

Wolfram turned. "Juanita, may I introduce the distinguished Dr. Timofey Karuchkin. Doctor, this is my equally distinguished colleague, Juanita. Be nice to her. She will save you."

Karuchkin bowed slightly, but said nothing.

"Where's Thome?"

"Down below near the reactor. He is writing a bookful of notes."

"You see, Doctor," Wolfram explained, "we brought along our own physicist to analyze your equipment. We didn't know we would . . . recover you."

"You haven't recovered me yet. And you'll need much

more than a simple external view of that reactor through the water to learn anything about it."

"Possibly. But we'll stay as long as we have to. Thome is an expert on isotope reactors, you see. He wants to study your neutron reflectors."

"Then he comprehends better than you that such knowledge is locked in here." He tapped his temple with a forefinger.

"Which brings me to an important question, Doctor. Will you go with us or stay here? Under the circumstances, we cannot force you. The decision is yours."

"There seems to be little choice. I'll go."

"This is going to be difficult for you, Juanita, but we'll have to shuttle Thome's air tanks and breathing gear back and forth to get us both out. Can you manage?"

"I believe so, yes. There should be plenty of air."

Wolfram turned to Karuchkin. "Of course, this means cutting short our man's inspection, Doctor. But I presume you can fill in the blanks."

Karuchkin shrugged.

"Juanita," Wolfram said, "what's happening on the outside? Any signs of Cinabre survivors? Desceau?"

"Nothing."

Wolfram was visibly relieved. "Desceau left here to go back to Atitlán. I wonder if he knows yet. What about it, Karuchkin?"

"I don't know. It is possible he knows about your attack on the power system. We have a radio antenna on the mountain. As for the flood, who knows?"

"What's he likely to do about the attack?"

"He will come with men and guns."

"How?"

"He might come in his floatplane."

"He couldn't land on the lake and he couldn't carry enough men."

[183]

"Overland, then. There is a good trail from Atranango, about fifty or fifty-five kilometers."

"That's a long hike."

"They have mules."

"Even moving at optimum," Wolfram calculated, "they couldn't be here before noon."

"Desceau will whip them along."

"Then we have to move quickly. All right, Juanita. Go ahead."

"I'll return as quickly as I can." She replaced her mask and mouthpiece, switched on her lantern, and slid back into the dark water.

II

A little less than an hour after Juanita had first made contact with Wolfram, they all sat, tired and wet, drying in the morning sun.

A few minutes later, the helicopter reappeared and they climbed aboard via the ladder. This time it was easier, for the floodwaters were slowly receding down across the shallower angle of the ridge.

But Karuchkin's presence required a change of plan. They could hardly return to Panajachel and risk a confrontation with Desceau and the Cubans. Nor was there enough fuel in the helicopter to fly directly into Guatemala City, where they could arrange a flight to smuggle the scientist out of the country. Consequently, after the pickup Wolfram ordered Kinsey to fly them to the high lake campsite while they worked the problem out.

It was near noon now. As they lounged comfortably around a fire, spooning rations, Wolfram quietly reviewed their options. The problem was twofold: Keep Karuchkin alive and well and smuggle him away, and evade Desceau and his minions.

[184]

"But you have not considered the one sure path to your survival," Karuchkin told them.

Wolfram glanced at him. "Enlighten us, Doctor."

"You must kill me, of course."

Thome was shocked. "Good Lord, Karuchkin, don't encourage them."

"I mean it." The physicist put his empty ration can down to one side. "We must look at this problem with total objectivity. As long as I live, I am first, an impediment, and second, a threat—either explicitly through some action of my own, or through recapture by the other side, wherein your basic mission is aborted."

"Very good, Doctor," said Magraw. "But you fail to balance those dangers against the gain for us."

Karuchkin laughed out loud. "So, you learn how my neutron reflectors work and you make gold. What does the United States need with such knowledge?" He rapped his spoon against a rock. "No! It is useless to a big power. Only a small country like Cuba could make effective use of such knowledge."

Wolfram chuckled. "So, the great Karuchkin is an economic theorist as well."

"Of course," Karuchkin said, "there is another alternative."

"Which is?"

"You could let me walk away." He waved his hand toward the hills. "Just wander over the mountain and leave me to my fate. After all, you have what you want. You have wrecked the reactor, destroyed Cinabre. Without me, you can escape Desceau and then, if your government orders it, come back and polish him off at your leisure."

"And you would just wander away over the hills?"

Karuchkin looked around the group. "Why not? Look, you have insurance. Just tell the KGB where you saw me. I could never go back to Cinabre."

When he received no response, he went on. "Desceau and

[185]

his minions even now must be in these hills seeking you. How long do you think you can last? And before too long they will have the gold machine working again."

Wolfram looked up at him sharply. "They'll have nothing but melted radioactive junk. Even now the water level is dropping. Soon there won't be enough to carry off the heat."

"All the more reason they will want *me*. Do you really think you can get out of Guatemala with me? They'll be looking everywhere. Especially the airports."

"That part's easy," said Kinsey.

"But the *reactor!*" Thome protested.

Kinsey laughed. "I'd love to see Desceau's face when that thing starts to melt after the water drains out. Instead of a gold machine, he'll have nothing but one big smoking, unapproachable lump somewhere down in the mountain."

"But that's just the *point*," Thome shouted in exasperation. "It *won't* melt down!"

"*Shut up!*" snarled Karuchkin.

Wolfram stared intently at Thome. "What are you saying?"

"It *won't* melt down. Our assumptions were incorrect."

"Explain!"

"Our plan was predicated on the assumption that the flood would drown the power system, short out all circuits."

"Correct. And that happened, except that Harada blew up one system. The water drowned out the other."

"But we assumed that the power stoppage would stop all of the safety systems. Therefore, when the water drained away, enormous heat would build up in the reactor and it would melt down."

"That was our assumption."

"Nevertheless," Thome went on, "while I was studying the reactor, I saw that all of the safety rods were still *in place*. Obviously, the safety circuits were able to work somehow and the rods moved in the correct position to prevent a meltdown."

"What the hell is this safety-rod stuff?" Kinsey wanted to know.

Thome explained. "The fission process within a nuclear reactor is controlled by moderators. These are rods containing neutron-absorbing substances that move through the fuel assemblies. In the Cinabre reactor this process serves two functions. First, it keeps the reactor from melting—like pushing a teaspoon up and down in a cup of hot coffee to cool it. Second, the neutron absorption converts the mercury to gold. But, any way you look at it, if the rods are not in place, there's nothing there to absorb the neutrons, and the reactor quickly becomes so hot it melts."

"What about it, Karuchkin?" Wolfram demanded. "Are the rods in place?"

The Russian smirked. "Your expert says they are. Who am I to argue?"

"They *are* in place," Thome repeated. "As long as they are, the reactor is safe. Nothing will happen."

Wolfram looked thoughtful. "Of course!" he exclaimed. "When the main power went out, the emergency system came on. It must have worked the safety shutdowns as well. That's it, isn't it?" Wolfram asked, staring at Karuchkin.

Karuchkin shifted uneasily but said nothing.

"Now it becomes clear," Magraw chuckled. "Karuchkin just wants us to kill him or let him walk away forever into the hills. A little peace, he says—that's all he wants." He pointed his finger at the Russian. "You were going to go right back to your reactor after all the dust settled and turn it back on again."

"Nonsense!" snapped Karuchkin.

"Not really," Wolfram observed. "It might be a long shot, but it would be a good one. Even now, there's probably a few hundred thousand in gold on the bottom of that lake—more than enough to get the power started again. As for Cinabre and Desceau . . . well, maybe he could accidentally irradiate them. . . ." He turned back to Thome. "This means we'll have to go back into Cinabre and get those rods out. Can it be done without cranes?"

"Probably. But it would be extremely dangerous. The radioactivity . . ."

"We have to risk it," said Wolfram gravely. "We'll find shielding in there. Something."

Karuchkin shook his head angrily. "You're fools! There could be enough gamma radiation there to destroy you in ten seconds."

"But, Doctor, *you're* going along."

Chapter Twenty-one

I

The lake was ebbing rapidly now, leaving behind it windrows of flotsam. The entrance to the Cinabre tunnel was exposed again, and currents of turbid water swirled out of it. There was no sign of life.

Kinsey brought the helicopter around once again while Wolfram scanned the opening and the surrounding terrain for some sign of Desceau. Behind them Karuchkin sat stoically, guarded by Magraw, who cradled one of the AKM's in his lap. The other rifle rested between Wolfram's knees. In the back of the craft were Thome, Juanita, and Harada.

Moments before, they had taken a short swing down the devastated gorge leading from the Gamma lake. The torrent had gouged one long, raw wound down the valley as far as the eye could see. The jungle lining its banks seemed to have been uprooted like handfuls of grass and tossed aside. Huge boulders had been tumbled from their bases and rolled and broken into jumbled, jagged patterns.

Nowhere was there any sign of a mule train or troops. Had they been on high ground they would have been seen. Had they been in the jungle, they were gone forever.

Wolfram signaled Kinsey to bring the helicopter down. The flier headed for the flat, water-covered tarmac area between the ridge and the original lake level. The craft hovered close to the surface. Wolfram motioned Karuchkin to open the door. They could get close enough to solid ground here that no ladder was needed. The physicist unfastened the latches and swung the door away. He sat down in the opening, then thrust himself out into the knee-deep water, which churned under the wind created by the rotors.

Magraw followed, with Wolfram covering him, then Thome. Wolfram was last out. He gave the thumbs-up sign to Kinsey, who took the aircraft up and away.

"When will they pick us up?" Thome asked anxiously.

"Later this afternoon," Wolfram replied, scanning the ridge again. Things seemed ominously quiet. It was a valley of the dead—or the waiting. "Kinsey's going to Panajachel for fuel. When they come back to pick us up, we're through with the Sierra de Flan."

"We hope," Magraw muttered.

"But we're not through yet," said Wolfram. "Karuchkin, lead the way."

The Russian turned and slogged through the littered water toward the Cinabre entrance. The others followed, Wolfram and Magraw with their rifles at the ready.

At the tunnel Karuchkin stopped and switched on his lantern. The others did the same. The Russian glanced at Wolfram.

"Proceed, Doctor. And please don't entertain any notions about weapons in case you trip over one."

Karuchkin waded ahead into the tunnel. The beams of their lanterns danced ahead in the blackness.

"You worry too much about me, Wolfram," Karuchkin called back. "What makes you think a physicist knows anything about handling firearms?"

"I read your dossier, Doctor. You were once in the Red Army."

"That was a long time ago."

"Obviously, you learned the lessons well. You're alive."

As they sloshed on against the drag of the outbound current, the plop and slap of water echoed from the exposed walls and ceiling. They might have been inside a tube of silver. Soon they came to the entry to the reactor chamber. The drowned Cuban was still there, now dangling grotesquely by his rifle sling, feet in the water, arms splayed.

"Thome," said Wolfram, "get that man's rifle and ammunition. We might need it."

The scientist froze.

"You don't have to touch him, Thome. Just get the weapon."

"I'll do it," Magraw volunteered.

The others focused their lights on the body as Magraw worked the AKM sling from its snag. The corpse rolled out of the strap and splashed into the water.

"No ammo pouches, Hugo."

"No? That's odd." He remembered the corpse floating there earlier as they had swum out of the mine, and could have sworn there were pouches attached. No matter, he thought, the mind plays tricks under such conditions.

"Don't the bullets get wet?" Thome asked.

"They're waterproofed," Wolfram told him. "They can be submerged for quite some time before the moisture seeps into the powder."

Magraw checked the rifle's magazine, then handed it to Thome. "It's loaded. This is the safety. It's on. You push it that way for firing. To shoot, you pull the trigger."

Thome accepted the rifle gingerly and slung it over his shoulder as they waded toward the reactor, now visible, shimmering inside its halo of radiation.

"Okay, Thome, what do we have to do to get those moderator rods out?"

"Before anything else, we must locate some shielding. Dr. Karuchkin, where are the protective garments kept?"

"Find them yourselves. I refuse to cooperate."

Wolfram brought the muzzle of his rifle around. "Really, Doctor, we must insist."

Karuchkin shrugged. "Over there. Those rows of lockers."

Inside the lockers, the leaden cloth suits had tumbled in

sodden heaps. They hauled the suits out and strung them awkwardly on the locker doors to drain.

"What's your plan, Thome?" Wolfram asked.

The physicist directed the beam of his lantern toward a crane above the reactor. From the crane dozens of cables threaded down to the top of the reactor. "The crane is out of service, of course. However, its function is to raise and lower the moderator rods together. We will have to raise the rods manually, by disconnecting each rod cable and splicing it to another rope or cable strung over the beams. Then, you and Magraw can haul in the cable, pulling the rods from the reactor individually. But we will have to act quickly."

"You just can't haul the rods out by hand?"

Thome shook his head. "Even underwater in the pool, the radiation from the emerging rods will be quite intense, especially if any of them should be mercury amalgam."

"Don't worry about that," Karuchkin muttered. "Those rods are boron replacements. We had not yet recharged with mercury."

"That's fortunate," said Thome. "In any event, we cannot risk the proximity required to remove the rods manually. It will have to be done from a distance."

"How will you know when the reactor goes critical?"

"There are a number of gauges around the pool." His light beam flashed across them.

"How fast will it happen?"

"We'll have time," Thome replied. "It will go critical at one precise moment. We remove another rod or two, then retreat. The water in the pool will dissipate much of the heat for a time."

"Bah!"

Magraw interjected, "Before we dress up, we'd better find some cable or rope to sling over the rafters. Also some wrenches and cable cutters."

"There's a toolroom down that side corridor"—Wolfram indicated with his light—"I saw some steel cable drums in there."

The others followed Karuchkin and Wolfram down the toolroom tunnel. There was no sign of Wolfram's guard, but near the tool cage entrance was another corpse, its muddy smock hooked over an electrical meter. The open eyes were filled with silt.

"This was my principal assistant," Karuchkin said tonelessly.

"A scientist?" Thorne asked.

Karuchkin nodded. "A scientist. A friend, perhaps. An able technician."

They turned from the body and waded into the tool cage, where the rush of water had upset bins and cabinets. The desk and chair had been tumbled to the other end of the area. Some of the wire fencing itself had been torn away. But along one side of the enclosure the heavy drums of cable were still in place.

"Here's a hand truck," said Magraw, pulling aside some fallen bins. "We can use it to wheel the cable down to the reactor." He trundled the small-wheeled carrier to one of the cable spools and wrestled it into position.

"Thorne, is there enough cable on that drum to do the job?" asked Wolfram.

"I think so. But we can come back for more if we need it."

"Excellent." Wolfram kicked aside debris until he found toolboxes with wrenches and cable-cutting equipment. "Will these wrenches work on the connections, Karuchkin?"

"Of course," the Russian murmured.

"Come on. We've got a lot of work and only a little time."

Magraw pushed the heavily laden hand truck out of the tool cage, plowing through the water. The others followed in his wake, holding their lanterns up to illuminate the way ahead.

Shortly, they were back in the reactor chamber, donning the heavy protective clothing.

"Our first job," said Thorne, "is to trail the cable up over the beams. Then we . . ."

Suddenly, a burst of laughter echoed all around them, a

[193]

disembodied, raucous sound with no discernible origin. Wolfram swung his lantern beam and rifle muzzle up in unison, but it was impossible to fix any target.

"Put it down, Hugo! Don't move an inch!"

Wolfram froze. So did the others.

"Now, very carefully, lean those rifles against the lockers."

They did so.

"Now put your lanterns on top of the lockers with the beams pointing straight out, then move away until I tell you to stop."

Silently, they followed the instructions.

"Karuchkin!" the voice boomed. "Take one of those AKMs and cover them."

The Russian obeyed quickly, stepping back into the shadows outside the light beams.

Now they heard the measured clang of footsteps descending a steel stairway. Wolfram knew it had to be the same one on which he and Karuchkin had taken refuge.

There was a soft splash and the sloshing sound of someone approaching through the water. A moment later a shape appeared in the light reflected from the lanterns.

"Never, never, try to make a fool of Harry Desceau."

II

For ten seconds the only sounds were the slap and gurgle of water. Then Desceau said, "Doctor, check them for weapons."

Karuchkin moved forward and patted them down deftly. He found nothing.

"So," Desceau said, "it was Firebird after all. You had me fooled for a while. The people here thought there was a whole platoon behind that attack. How many did you have?"

"One."

"*One?*"

"One of my men."

"Who?"

"He's not here right now. But he and the others are outside now. Put aside that rifle and maybe we can talk a deal. Save us all a lot of trouble."

"Ha!" Desceau sneered. "Not a chance. You couldn't *dream* up a deal I'd give a nickel for."

Time, thought Wolfram, we have to buy some time. To Desceau he said, "Let me try. What have you got to lose by listening?"

Desceau smiled. "I like your style, Wolfram. So I'll let you talk. A few closing remarks, so to speak."

Wolfram took a deep breath before he spoke. "My people know all about Cinabre. Everything. If I don't check back in with them, they'll start a follow-up and Cinabre's days are numbered. But there *is* another way."

Desceau's face registered no response.

"Play ball with us," Wolfram pleaded. "We buy up the Cinabre stock that's available on the bourses. Together with your stock we have a majority. We vote the Cubans out and put our people in."

Desceau frowned. "You and your crowd have been nothing but trouble."

At least I have his attention, thought Wolfram. And a little time. "It could turn the other way," he said to Desceau. "It happens all the time. What have you got to lose?"

"The problem with your idea, my friend, is that it depends on us all trusting each other. And, frankly, we don't, do we?" Desceau looked around at the Firebird group. As he did, his face relaxed into a smile. "I'm really rather sorry about this, you know. It's so terribly messy."

He brought the AKM slowly up to his shoulder. The motion seemed incredibly slow. Desceau's eyes were expressionless in the half-light of the lanterns.

The muzzle came up.

BUH-BUH-BUPP!!!

The shots crashed around the vast chamber, slamming and ricocheting against the walls.

Desceau seemed startled by the sounds. His hands opened spastically, and the AKM fell into the water. Then his eyes rolled back and he collapsed.

"Karuchkin!" cried Thome.

They turned toward the Russian. He stood woodenly, the rifle butt under his right arm. A thin loop of smoke coiled from the muzzle, twining upward through the lantern beams.

Epilogue

I

If Mr. Julio Sanchez was disconcerted with all of these new instructions, he did not question them. His job was to smooth the paths of commerce between differing cultures, economic persuasions, and political philosophies.

Therefore, when his contacts in the Cinabre Corporation ordered a pair of 3,500-horsepower, opposed-piston diesel engines for immediate delivery, prepaid, by air carrier in Guatemala City, he implemented the order promptly, and the detailed contracts were signed expeditiously. It was not a particularly unusual transaction.

What *was* unusual was the channel of finance.

As was his usual practice, Sanchez arranged his lines of credit through certain specific foreign banks or insurance organizations, nebulous sources, at best. Arrangements always were verbal, but Sanchez was comfortable with them because they worked.

But this new line of credit was through an American bank with an odd name that he had difficulty remembering. The Cinabre instructions were quite firm.

Sanchez didn't like dealing with American banks. They had a disappointing way of cooperating with Federal authorities on confidential matters.

Then there was the gold business.

For some unfathomable reason, all of the gold futures contracts previously sold on American exchanges had to be repurchased, at no small loss, and then resold on the foreign exchanges. It was puzzling to Sanchez. It was almost as if Cinabre had no interest in speculating against the U.S. dollar, but was interested only in foreign currencies. Sanchez wondered why.

What *was* the name of that bank? He rummaged through his folder and extricated a piece of correspondence on letterhead stationery.

Of course.

The Grain Exchange & Merchants Trust.

II

Ultimately, disposition of the matter had been taken care of by the Bank.

But the form of the matter had been determined by Dr. Karuchkin. After all, he held the gun.

After Desceau fell, the three Firebird men faced the Russian with a mixture of relief and fear. The immediate threat was gone, but the muzzle of the physicist's AKM was pointed at them.

"So," Wolfram said finally. "You've opted to join us."

"Not quite."

"What, then?"

"Let us talk. You made a proposal to him." He nodded at the body. "It interested me."

Wolfram's eyes narrowed. "The idea was that he—and you, of course—take over Cinabre with our people. Throw the Cubans out."

Karuchkin nodded. "I know it was desperate, but there was the germ of an idea in it."

"Go ahead."

"First allow me to review some realities."

"By all means."

"One reality is that *you* and your people, whoever they are, know all about the Cubans and Cinabre."

[198]

"Correct."

"But, for their part, the Cubans, too, know all about Cinabre and they undoubtedly now know about you." Karuchkin frowned. "Consequently, Wolfram, I think your proposal to Desceau was flawed."

"That's probable."

"Therefore," Karuchkin went on, "we can conclude that even if you chose to operate Cinabre, with or without Desceau, the Cubans eventually would destroy it to keep it from you."

Wolfram nodded.

"But, for your part," Karuchkin continued, "you intend even now to destroy Cinabre to keep it from the Cubans."

"And," said Wolfram, "the fact that you are holding that AKM alters neither of those conclusions."

"It may," said the Russian. "There is a third alternative."

"What?"

Karuchkin smiled. "Make an agreement with the Cubans. Operate Cinabre jointly, for your mutual benefit."

Even Thome joined in the laughter.

"Ridiculous!" said Wolfram, shaking his head.

"I accept your superficial reaction, your laughter," Karuchkin said seriously. "With the Cubans it would be the same. But it can be done."

"I think he means it," said Magraw.

"Look at the realities," the physicist went on. "One side cannot let the other have this system alone. At the same time, the world cannot be allowed to know of the Cinabre gold, for economic reasons. This is agreed to by all. Yet, the only way to preserve this secret is for those who know it to agree among themselves to keep it, isn't that so?"

Wolfram studied him thoughtfully. "There is some sense there, Karuchkin. Let's hear the rest of it."

"At this moment there are only three living Cubans who know in detail what Cinabre is about, all members of the Cinabre board of directors, all here in Guatemala. They could be assembled in Atitlán quickly. All that you must do, Wolfram,

[199]

is contact your principals and bring them to the same place. Let them talk."

"What about him?" Wolfram nodded at Desceau's corpse. "What happens to his shares of Cinabre, his house by Lago Atitlán? There'll be questions."

Karuchkin shrugged. "We have here the corpse of a man who was killed by guerrillas. His property legally belongs to his company, Cinabre."

Wolfram nodded slowly and turned to Magraw. "Am I numb with shock, or does this idea make sense?"

"It's worth a try. Talk to the Bank."

"All right," Wolfram said to the Russian. "We'll take it up with our people. You understand, of course, that their reaction might be negative."

"I understand."

"What now?"

"Leave Dr. Thome with me as hostage while you proceed as you must. If your response is favorable, I will contact the Cubans."

The meetings were held in the main room of the late Harry Desceau's house overlooking Lago Atitlán.

The Bank agreed.

The Cubans agreed.

Gold 200.